MW00987459

REDEMPTION
IN THE TAHOE BASIN

Book 3

S. S. DUSKEY

Printed in the United States of America
First printing, 2022
Cover images by D. Driggers
Cover design and author photo by D. Driggers
Editor - Carrie Padgett
Publishing Coordinator - Sharon Kizziah-Holmes

SakiRose Publishing
Hamilton, MT

www.ssduskeyauthor.com
ssduskey@yahoo.com

ISBN - 13:978-0-578-39212-7

DEDICATION

This book is dedicated to Lillian Weinstock, a.k.a. Mamma Lil. Thank you for your love, inspiration, and for being my number one fan. You are missed.

ACKNOWLEDGEMENTS

I would like to thank Steve Weinstock, Jon Eubanks, Teri Albrecht, Charisse Rose, Julia Grimes, and Herman Hill for their expertise in their respective fields.

A special note of appreciation to Andy and Melissa with AV8-Orr for the use of their helicopter.

PROLOGUE

"**M**ayday, mayday, mayday! Four, seven, eight, Charlie-Bravo. Cessna 210 with engine failure. Attempting forced landing. Current position seven miles southwest of Tiger Field." The fifty-four-year-old eased back on the throttle. "Teddy Reagan, pull out of this. You are not dying today," he uttered through gritted teeth.

Teddy switched fuel tanks and turned the boost pump to high, but the engine sputtered and the plane violently shook as it lost power. His altitude was slipping.

"Tiger tower, acknowledge!" No response. His stomach churned. He switched to emergency frequency 121.5. "Mayday, mayday, mayday. Four, seven, eight, Charlie-Bravo. Does anyone copy?!" More dead air. All communication was lost. The pilot commenced emergency landing procedures he'd run through hundreds of times in simulators. The Centurion continued to descend as fast as his pummeling heart.

"Going down in the desert," he shouted, hoping someone—anyone—would hear his broadcast. The desert drew closer, and his stall horn began blaring. With the landing gear up, he eased the yoke to raise the nose. He held his breath as the tail hit first. Momentum took over, and the Centurion somersaulted, over and over, finally landing upright. The windshield blew in as sand and sagebrush exploded in the cockpit.

Teddy's aviators and headset flew off as he slammed forward on the instrument panel and snapped back to the headrest.

He sat with eyes closed for a spell then blinked them open. "What the hell!" His vision was blurry, but he knew the smiling faces greeting him were his three beautiful daughters. And one ultra-sound. Photographs clipped to the plane's sun shield.

He glanced around the cockpit and groaned at the throbbing pain in his face and the back of his neck.

"I'm alive!" He clutched his head. Teddy peered down as bright red streaks trickled onto his white-collared shirt. With his bloody, trembling, sweat-soaked hands, he raised the latch, releasing the seat belt and shoulder harness, but it was stuck. He slammed it with his fist. It was a matter of time before his plane went up in a fiery blaze. Just as the distinct odor of Avgas grew stronger, the harness released, and he was freed. "Thank you, God." He gazed to the heavens.

Teddy snatched the pictures of his family and placed them in the inside pocket of his canvas vest and grabbed his .38 Smith and Wesson from the side pouch of the plane. The moment he shoved the gun in his black leather flight jacket pocket, smoke billowed from the engine. He slithered out as the Cessna caught fire then army crawled as quick as his injured body allowed on the harsh thorny desert surface. He watched as lizards and jack rabbits scampered out of harm's way. But kept his head on a swivel for rattlers.

He made his way to a desert rock formation, half the size of his plane, and took cover. Teddy slumped against the bolder and lamented at his torching Cessna. Suddenly, a burning pain seared through his lower body. He glanced and noticed a three-inch wide laceration on his left thigh. He removed a handkerchief from his jacket pocket and applied pressure, wincing with every compression.

As he let out a pained yelp, it occurred to him the date was May first. *May Day*. Teddy shook his head at the cruel irony and pondered as he leaned back, his face absorbing the noon sun. There was not a cloud in the sky. It was a comfortable seventy-two degrees and perfectly smooth flying conditions. So, if Mother Nature was not the cause of his crash, it must've been sabotaged. "Contaminated fuel," he said with a snarl.

Just as he contemplated his next move, the whizzing of helicopter rotors loomed. The orange Bell 206 buzzed him like a bird and soared above. He blew out a sigh of relief. The timing couldn't have been better as he grew weaker from the blood loss. He was saved. His heart fluttered at the twinge of excitement of meeting his new grandbaby.

Teddy waved his arms high in the air and shouted. "Over here, over here!" He braced for the chopper to land, but it didn't. The chopper's pilot flew adjacent to the wrecked Cessna and kicked up dust and sagebrush. He threw his arms up in a failed attempt to shield his face from the swirling desert debris. Then the chopper slipped away as swiftly as it appeared.

"What the ... hey, hey." He yelled again and flailed his arms. Didn't they see him? Teddy lowered his shoulders and stroked his pulsating head. And then it hit him harder than the crash. A gut-wrenching thought. It was *them*. They found him and would return. The nausea rippled in his stomach.

"They can't find it." Teddy hastily scanned the desert floor. He'd risked his life and his family's for the information. A decision he regretted. A few minutes later, he heard tires crunching beneath the sand. As they drew closer, he removed his black leather strapped watch and pulled out the pictures from his inside pocket and kissed them. Teddy tucked the photos in the band and placed them in an alcove in the boulder. He secured them with a couple of jagged, heavy rocks.

Just as his enemies' black GMC was in sight, he pulled his iPhone from his front pocket. Although it was cracked, he tapped the record button. "Don't know if you'll get this ... service bad." His speech was breathy. "They found me, family not safe. Violet Protocol. I repeat Violet Protocol ... I love you all and I'm sorry." With tears in his eyes, he faced the camera toward the rock outcropping and zoomed on the pictures with the watch, panning to the plane and back. "I'll be *watching*." Teddy waited for the video to send and smashed the phone against the desert floor.

He staggered to his feet, using the divots in the boulder as if he were a rock climber, and dragged his lean six foot two, battered, drenched body toward his torching plane, away from the rock outcropping and the photos. Teddy teetered as he stood tall. The intense heat emitting from the crash enveloped him.

The dust from the approaching vehicle loomed over him and two male passengers swiftly exited. "Over there," one of them shouted.

Teddy pulled the .38 from his pocket. His hand trembled beneath the grip. He made the sign of the cross.

Pop ... pop ... pop.

CHAPTER 1

Two days later.

My heart pounded with each thrust of my arms. Sweat dripped into my plain black sports tankini and my high ponytail tossed about as Van Halen's "Panama" blared in my ear buds. The energetic rock music gave me the motivation to finish my quick five miles on the treadmill. It wasn't my usual scene for running, but I was at a three-day conference in Napa and at five in the morning I didn't feel like pounding the pavement.

I was determined to burn off last night's high caloric intake. My best friend from college, Siui Sullivan, drove up from San Diego to help me celebrate my promotion. Parole Agent II, finally. Her family, like mine, was of Irish lineage. Siui's name meant Rose, but since it was impossible to spell, let alone pronounce, she just went by "Sue."

Back in our college days, Sue and I were mistaken for twins. We were born the same year. Both stood five feet, eight inches, and roughly one-hundred and twenty-five pounds. I had long, wavy red hair, hers was to her shoulders. Our blue eyes were also a shade off one another, mine were sapphire, Sue's a sky blue. But we both had legs for miles.

After an evening of wine tasting, carbtastic Italian food, and karaoke, I insisted she stay the night. In our poor college days, we'd shared many a king-sized bed. Sue was still crashed out upstairs in my hotel room when I crept out. As I reflected on last night's shenanigans, my face and side still ached from laughing, something I hadn't done in over a year. Life was good. I chuckled, shaking my head.

As I amped my volume and speed for the final stretch, a woman, roughly my age, mid-thirties, entered the compact hotel gym, carrying a white towel. She wore a plain gray, hooded sweatshirt, non-descript blue jeans, black tactical boots, and a black baseball cap with Safariland embroidered on the lid. She gave me a nod as she dropped her towel on my fanny pack holster. I studied her and was ready to pounce since it contained my new pistol, Springfield, Hellcat 9mm and badge wallet.

The woman picked up the towel. As she swiftly exited, I noted she carried a mild limp. I dismissed her as someone from the conference who was probably looking to use the only treadmill in the gym that I occupied. But in her street clothes and tactical boots?

As the next chorus played, a text interrupted my groove. I slowed my speed and grabbed my iPhone off the top of the treadmill. The message was from an unknown number. *T's compromised, family in danger, leave hotel now!*

The only person who sent cryptic messages was my Grandma Lil, former CIA. I'd been waiting on word of Teddy's—or as she referred to him as "T's"—whereabouts. Teddy went dark a few weeks ago.

"This can't be good," I mumbled, hitting the red stop button on the treadmill. As it slowed, I hopped off, snatched a white hotel towel from the rack, and wiped the sweat from my neck and chest. I grabbed my fanny pack and stared. What appeared to be a burner phone was under it. I picked it up and scanned the room. There was only one other gym rat this early using the facility and he was in his own world.

"What the—" I snapped the pack on my waist and hustled out of the gym, hoping to get a visual on the mystery woman who'd left it. I stuffed the burner phone in the left side pocket of my black running leggings, jamming my iPhone in the right.

I searched for the gal and ignored my grandmother's warning. Something I was very good at doing. I jetted up the stairs to my room on the third floor. I flung open the entry door and immediately saw two men, dressed in all black, fleeing from my room at the far end of the hall. Both at least six feet. The hair on the nape of my neck stood on end.

"Hey ... what the hell are you doing?" I shouted and raced after them with my hand on my pack, ready to draw my weapon.

The men slipped out the exit door without looking back.

I sprinted the length of the hall and threw the exit door wide. I hurtled down a flight of stairs to the second-floor landing, peering up and down the stairwells, but the men vanished.

I shot back to my floor and the moment I re-entered the hallway, I observed the door to my room was ajar with the hotel privacy latch. With my left hand, I ripped the drawstring of my fanny pack and drew my pistol with my right, keeping it at a high ready position. I slammed against the door with the full weight of my body and hugged the wall as I entered. My training kicked in and I was ready to clear the room for any intruder left behind, or so I'd thought.

I stood with my mouth agape and clutched my stomach as nausea rushed through me.

CHAPTER 2

"Sue!" I shouted and quickly scanned the room with my pistol and dashed to the bed where she lay on her stomach. She had what appeared to be a 40-caliber sized hole in the back of her head. Her eyes bulged wide with a shocked, bloody expression on her face. The white hotel sheets were crimson soiled.

"No ... no ... no ... God, no!" I jammed the weapon into my pack and dropped to my knees. I knew she was gone, but I checked for a carotid pulse. My knees buckled as I stood, and my hands trembled as I wrenched the iPhone from my pocket. As I dialed 911 and waited for the dispatcher, I glanced around my blood splattered hotel room and noticed they tossed it like a Caesar Salad.

"911, what is your emergency?" dispatch answered, calm and even.

"My fr—" The words could not pass my lips. I've seen my share of murdered people over my career, but never someone this close to me.

"Ma'am, please repeat yourself," the operator steadily replied.

I drew a deep, painful breath as I paced with my palm to my forehead. "There's be—"

The door flung open and hit the wall as the woman with the Safariland baseball cap grabbed the cell from my grasp, disconnected the call and powered down the phone.

"What the hell!" I snatched the phone back, stuffed it in my pocket.

"Shh ... lower your voice." She put her finger to her lips as she closed the door.

"Who are you?" I jumped back, fists up, ready for a fight. The woman stood nearly six feet with a much larger build. I sized her up, wondering how it was going to play out.

She waved her hands as she advanced closer. "Easy, Agent O'Brien. I'm here to help," she said with a strong Bostonian accent. "But we gotta go ... now."

I stepped back and pulled my gun. "How do I know you're not here to finish the job?" I jutted my chin to Sue's body.

"Trust me, Rose, you wouldn't have seen me coming," she said, raising her arms just above her waist. "My name is Copper. And your grandmother's friend sent me. If you don't believe me, look at the burner."

With my eyes trained on her, I held her at

gunpoint with my right hand. I yanked the burner phone out with my left, bringing it to eye level, and glanced at it. Sure enough. Grandma Lil verified her story.

"Who did this to my friend? **And why didn't you snatch me in the gym?**" My voice shook as I re-holstered my gun into the pouch and pocketed the phone.

"There was another guy there … and no time to chat. Follow me," she said as she clutched my elbow.

I reared my head and scowled. "I'm not leaving her. I'm a person of interest and will need to talk to the cops."

She grabbed my shoulders. "Rose, that was supposed to be you."

I threw her hands off me. "Don't touch me!" I said through gritted teeth.

"Sorry, but they have to think you're dead."

"Who the hell are *they*?" I asked.

"Later. But your entire family's been compromised. We gotta go." Copper walked over to the door, opened it, and peeked her head out, scanning both directions. "What do ya think they'll do when they've discovered they got the wrong target?" She snapped a look at me over her shoulder. "*Everyone* has to think you're dead … for now … and leave your phone off. They can track you." Copper removed her baseball cap and shook her short, curly, reddish-brown hair, running her fingers through it. She handed it to me. "Put it on."

I gripped the hat. "**That's flippin' fantastic,**" I said. "Wait! Not my family. My sister is seven months pregnant."

"Don't worry ... your grandma will handle it."

Tears welled as I stared at Sue. I considered. "We can't leave her here ... like this." I gulped hard as my bottom lip quivered.

"I have someone on it." Copper waved me toward the door. "Put on the damn hat," she said, narrowing her hazel eyes.

I threw it on, sliding my ponytail through the opening in the back and grabbed the first item of clothing, a plain black zipped hooded sweatshirt. I shrugged into it as we crept out. We exited out the side where the assassins fled and bolted down two flights. My head on a swivel for anyone dressed in all black. As I followed Copper, I spotted a bulge in her waistband. Most likely a gun. Copper was right. She could've popped me and I wouldn't have seen it coming.

Copper used a card key to gain entrance to a restricted employee area. Who was she? I studied her as we made our way through the door. We slowed our gait and nodded to employees milling about, preparing for their morning shift. She suddenly jerked me into an alcove. "There's a white Yukon Denali with no plates, blacked-out windows parked outside this door." She whispered. "The driver's name is Mia. Hop in the back and duck down. She'll drive ya outta here."

"What about you?" I said with crossed arms.

"I've gotta clean house ..." Copper peered past me as she scanned the room. "And get you off the hook. I know a guy, he works Homicide. He's on his way. I'm sure that other guy in the gym can be your alibi. Now go!"

The first thing my mother taught me was never to take rides from strangers. I squinted. Especially not knowing the identities of the hit men.

CHAPTER 3

My stomach churned as sirens wailed closer. As a parole agent, I ran *to* crime scenes, not fled them. I started for the employee exit and peeked over my shoulder. The second Copper limped out of sight, I hurried through the kitchen and out the back door.

Damn it! I had my state vehicle but left my keys upstairs. Oh well, I couldn't be caught driving it. I dug through my pack and found Sue's key fob. I drove her Land Rover to the hotel last night since she drank too much.

The moment I exited, I shuddered as the early morning temperature chilled through me. I flipped the hood over my hat and lowered my gaze and waited as cops swarmed the hotel, their red and blue lights flashing, converging from every direction. When all was clear, I headed for the Rover, slid behind the wheel, and pressed start, speeding toward my haven, Grass Valley.

I zipped down I-12 to Interstate 80 East. If my soul wasn't crushed, I would've enjoyed the pale dark blue and pink sun peeking up from the skyline. But it was gray and sunless to me as Sue's bloody face was branded into my frontal lobe. "Who ... what? I don't understand." Tears gushed down my cheeks and clouded my vision. I wiped them away.

After a half hour on the road, I pulled out my iPhone, powered it on and then remembered it could and was most likely being tracked. I immediately shut it off, took out the burner, and called Grandma Lil. It went straight to voicemail.

Hello, you have reached Violet. I am unavailable right now. You know what to do.

"Violet?!" I shouted, swerving into the next lane, cutting off the driver. He laid on his horn and gave me a middle finger salute.

That recording meant one thing. She'd gone dark and would have to contact *me.* Hence the burner. My heart quivered at the mention of "Violet," my mother's name.

After I reunited with my grandmother in Montana, she schooled me and my sisters on her secret life in the CIA and Teddy's. Since we were in the know, she concluded we needed a family safety protocol if there was a security breach. If the word "Violet" was mentioned outside of referring to my mother, Grandma would go on a technological lockdown and use a backdoor, archaic system until she swept it clean. And the family would flee to the closest safe house.

As I pondered *why* we were compromised, Teddy came to mind. He was in the middle of acquiring damaging information on high profile, perilous people. I slammed my steering wheel and clenched my jaws. The entire morning reeked of my father. On the drive home, I rehearsed what I'd say to him, when and *if I* ever saw Teddy again.

I drove the back way through Yuba City, taking side streets and detouring to the main highway, keeping an eye out for a tail. Being suspicious was second nature to me. The two-hour drive was closer to two and a half. Lucky for me, the commuter traffic was light for a Tuesday morning.

As I pulled into Grass Valley, it occurred to me the second part of the Violet Protocol was that I *wasn't* to return home, but head straight for the safe house in Homewood. "Crap ... too late now," I muttered.

It was 8:05 a.m. when I arrived in my sleepy, rustic neighborhood. All the houses were at least a couple of acres apart and heavily forested with oaks and pine trees. I crept down my street and just as I was two rural blocks away, I spotted the Denali, no plates, blacked-out windows. They'd parked a few houses from mine on the opposite side of the street.

They couldn't have beaten me by much, even with my doubling back and detours.

I cut my engine, exited, and gently shut the Rover's door, putting the key fob in my pouch. An early morning shiver sliced through me again, so I zipped my sweatshirt to my neck. Only to discover I'd unintentionally grabbed Sue's. I sighed. "Suck it up, Rose. Focus," I said, adjusting the hood over Copper's hat.

With my eyes trained on my target, I drew the pistol from my pack. I lowered my center of gravity and moved heel to toe in a steady and smooth stride. I looked like Groucho Marx walking in the shadows. The SUV was idling next to the curb, and the windows were halfway down. The closer I got, I heard the two gals chatting in an inaudible murmur.

I popped my head from outside the passenger window and drew down on them.

"Show me your hands ... both of you ... *now*!" I barked.

CHAPTER 4

Saki lounged on a brown leather La-Z-Boy recliner in the living room of their rented Fort Lauderdale town home, rubbing her enormous belly, sipping orange juice. She followed her husband with her eyes as he paced a hole in the carpet of the Florida room, smoothing his mustache and flailing his arms as he spoke in his earbuds. It was his day off and he should be relaxing. Instead, he looked ready to choke whoever was on the other end of the conversation.

James disconnected the call, opened the sliding glass door, and stepped inside. He stood with fists on his hips. "How does Rose get into so much damn trouble? I mean, it's only eleven in the morning ... well, eight in California," he said, slipping the phone into his back jean's pocket.

Saki picked up a jar that read *Swear Jar/College Fund-3 of 3* and held it to him.

"Not now, honey, this is serious." He grabbed the jar and placed it on the white granite breakfast bar. His round brown eyes grew larger than normal.

"Okay, Mr. Powers, what's going on? You didn't call her Felicity." Saki lowered the recliner. She rolled side to side like a turtle on its shell, grunting to a stand. Her long, golden locks were in a high ponytail and flipped with each movement.

James helped his very pregnant wife to her feet. "Yeah, I reserve that nickname when she is *not* in a whole heap of trouble." His six-foot frame towered over her by five inches as he kissed her forehead. "You know how I promised never to keep anything from you? But you're eight months pregnant and don't need the stress."

"Seven, that's what we told everyone." Saki dragged her head backward and furrowed her brows. "Is Rose okay?" she asked.

"I just got off the phone with my friend, the one who works on the 3rd floor at her department headquarters." He pursed his lips and shook his head. "Rose is missing."

"What? Ho—why? I don't understand. I spoke to her last night. She's in Napa at a work thing with her old college friend, Sue. They called from a wine bar. It was nice to hear her laughing," Saki said.

"Not anymore. They discovered Sue's body in Rose's hotel room. She'd been shot in the back of the head. Execution style."

Saki watched as he paced like a worried father. She plopped on the arm of the chair. "I ... I can't believe this," she said, stifling a sob.

"This is bad. Rose is not answering her phone, and they found her state car in the parking lot of the hotel." James smoothed his crew cut chestnut brown hair. "They're sending someone to her house to check on her," he said.

"Wait! They don't suspect her, do they?" Saki asked.

"No, that's what's peculiar. A homicide detective cleared her of any involvement without even interviewing her. Right now, she's just AWOL."

"She would never go absent without leave. It's not like her." Saki stood again and waddled to the bar. She rummaged through her purse and removed her cell and scrolled through looking for the tracking app. "Hmm, Rose still has not accepted my request to follow her. I'm not surprised. And her phone is off." She stared at her cell. "Can't you track her phone?" she asked.

"Not without a warrant and even then, it'll take a while, unless ... you have secret squirrel connections." James pulled the cell from his pocket and called another number.

"Who are you calling?" Saki asked.

"The squirrel," James said, "she should be able to help." He raised his brows and rubbed his forehead as he disconnected the call. He mouthed, *shh,* and put his finger to his lips. "Hey, babe, are you ready to go buy paint for the baby's room?" He nodded toward the front door as he picked up Saki's purse off the breakfast bar.

Saki cocked her head, snatched her swear jar, and followed him outside.

"What in the hel—uh, heck?" Saki said.

James hustled his wife to his FBI government G-ride, a black Chevy Tahoe. "Your grandmother's outgoing message said 'Violet' was not available," he whispered in her ear.

Saki slid into the passenger seat and clicked her belt. "Oh ... this is bad. Really bad. Where are we going?"

"Palm Island. My mother's house. I know the renovations are not complete, but it's under the radar," James said. "I'll have someone drive me back later to fetch your vehicle and pack some clothes. The important thing is to get you to safety."

Saki let out a whimper and slumped, her head in her hands.

"Don't worry, Rose is okay ... she is resourceful and has been through worse," James said as he grabbed Saki's hand.

"I know ... but look at me? I'm a walking billboard for Pepto Bismol. I look like a pink whale. I didn't think I was going anywhere today and threw on ... this." Saki cried and gestured to herself. "I'm not exactly dressed for *Palm Island*."

"You look beautiful, mother of my child," James said.

"Easy for you to say. At least you're wearing designer jeans, a polo shirt and Dockers." She peered at her feet. "Not these silly starfish flip flops." She blew her nose. "Sorry, my emotions are getting carried away. Rose *has* to be okay ... wait. What about Kaylee? She's on her way from Jacksonville. Someone needs to get her. Is Kevin available?"

"O'Malley's on vacation. He's in South Lake Tahoe at a bachelor party. I'll get someone else," James said.

"I'd feel better if Kevin was aware of the situation." Saki looked at James with watery eyes.

"I'll contact him. Don't worry those beautiful blues, darlin'." He stroked her cheek. "And with Kevin being so close, he should be able to help," James said.

Saki rubbed her belly and gazed at the clear blue sky. "Why can't we have a normal family?" she asked with a heavy sigh, wiping her tears.

CHAPTER 5

Max Ryan sat on the upper deck of his 186 Delta Superyacht, equipped with a helipad and boat garage. The yacht was anchored off the Mazatlán shore. It was one of his many assets the feds did not seize. He continued his morning ritual of getting natural vitamin D, without causing too much skin damage. He basked shirtless and offered his chiseled face and six foot three, one-hundred-and-eighty-pound frame to the seventy-degree sun.

Max placed his iPhone on the mahogany deck table and put the call on speaker.

"Are you sure you want to leave your trust to one person?" inquired a man with a New York accent.

"Yes. My mother would've wanted it that way," Max replied.

"Okay. What about the funds in the other

account? The one your uncle left. You are the only heir," the man said.

"I transferred it to my mother's foundation," Max said.

"Yes, I was told you were a magician with making money disappear and clean. Let's see ..." Max listened as the man leafed through papers. "Found it, uh ... the Vivian Alexander Foundation?"

"Yes." Max shouldered into his **Italian**-made white Brioni linen shirt, leaving it open for the breeze to cool him. He opened his laptop computer and was down to business, checking emails.

"As your new trust attorney, I need to get something straight. Maxwell Ryan is your legal name, correct? Not Samuel Alexander."

Max rolled his head. He had not heard Samuel, a.k.a. Sammy Alexander, mentioned in a long time. A twinge developed. "I am Max Ryan. My dad was Maxwell."

"Okay, but your birth name was Samuel Alexander? And you changed it after you were released from juvenile hall?"

Max narrowed his cerulean eyes at the phone. "Wait ... how did you find out? My records were sealed," he said, running hands through his freshly washed raven hair with the latest Gerard Butler haircut.

"It's right here in my father's notes. You remember my father was your parents' attorney? There's a notation indicating your birth name was Samuel Alexander."

"If you mention Samuel Alexander again,

you're fired. Am I clear?" Max flared his nostrils as he drew a deep, meditated breath.

"Uh … yes. Yes, Sir. Uh … Okay, so Thomas Marchetti? Never legally existed?" The man's voice shook.

"Correct. It was an assumed name to get me back into the states. Something I hope to never do *again*. I am Max Ryan. Now we've got that clear. Can we proceed?" he said in a low growl.

"Yes, Si—"

Max's iPhone beeped with an incoming call. The caller ID read *Chena Fin*. He expelled a loud sigh and pressed *Decline*.

Max met Chena for the first time six months ago in Montana. She was an attorney by trade, but as of late worked as an art advisor for questionable and dangerous employers. He knew ignoring her would displease her, but he didn't care.

"Send over the documents. I'll sign and have my staff return it," Max replied.

"Mr. Ryan, Sir. This must be signed in person at my office, at once. If something were to happen to you, the government gets it *all*. There is a lot of money."

Max glared at his cell as another call from Chena came through. He declined it again. "Did you *not* hear me? I am *never* returning to the states. And besides, nothing is going to happen to me before we get the paperwork done." Max flicked his wrist in a dismissive fashion as if the man could see him.

"Sir, no one is bullet proof. And this is a lot o—"

"I know ... a lot of money. Fine, I have a notary on my staff. We'll do it *my* way. Am I clear? You'd have to drag me by gunpoint back to the states," Max said, sipping his cucumber infused water.

"I just sent the trust. It should be in your e-mail. But I need the originals," the attorney urged.

"I will handle it." Max disconnected the call and snapped his fingers.

A tall, red-haired Latina deckhand was there on a dime. "Si, señor," she said. She wore a white polo and matching skort, and deck shoes. She stood with her hands behind her back and head up.

Max perused his emails and found the one from his attorney and hit print.

"Get the document off my printer and bring it to me. Have Javier bring his notary supplies. He needs to send this immediately," Max ordered.

"Si." She spun on her heels and marched away.

Max's cell rang. He rolled his head, snatched the phone, and hit the red button for the third time. An immediate text came through with an attachment. *Answer, NOW!* it read. Max shrugged it off.

Seven missed calls from Chena and forty-five minutes later, the last notarized signature was complete. Max's cell pinged with an e-mail and attachment again. He opened it on his computer and studied it with wide eyes. The picture was of a woman with a hole through her head. He gasped and his heart skipped a beat.

He stared at the sea and returned his attention to the photo and zoomed in. "Wait a minute," he spoke to the computer. He wore a Cheshire cat grin. The deceased woman had shoulder length red hair, a shade red off of Rose's, not to mention the faded barbed wire tattoo on her wrist.

Max held his arms close to his pounding chest as he ran his hand along the scars on his abdomen where his beloved Rose shot him a year ago while they were in the Florida Keys. He then examined his right arm where her bullet grazed him six months ago. Scarred reminders of her.

"My Rose is fierce. She would never go down that easy." He reared his head and let out a loud guffaw. "Nice try, Chena," he mumbled.

In the distance, he heard *whop, whop, whop, whop*. Max glared at the incoming chopper. He instantly regretted allowing D.O.G. and Lucy to fly off on his helicopter with his armed men.

Max's phone rang again. This time he answered.

CHAPTER 6

Teddy Reagan jarred awake to a boot to his rib, followed by a florescent blaze. "Argh," he grimaced through gritted teeth. He shielded his eyes with his hands from the blinding light. Through a slit in his left eye, Teddy spotted a long metal chain with a hook dangling from the ceiling. As he stirred, the concrete floor chilled beneath him. He was in a cold, damp basement with no exterior windows. The smell of death hung in the air. A tidal wave of nausea rushed through him.

The wounded pilot rolled to his side. "Ahh!" he shouted again. Although he'd survived the plane crash, there were new radiating twinges throughout his entire body, definitely not caused by the accident. What had they done to him? He felt along his right eye where it was complete darkness. His heart raced. Did he still have his eyeball? He breathed a sigh of relief when he pried it open with his fingers. He imagined he looked like someone who'd gone a round or two with the Irish cage fighter, Conor McGregor.

Just as he adjusted his vision with his good eye, he spied a pair of black steel-toed boots clacking against the floor, ready to give him another wallop. He grabbed the foot and grumbled.

"Wake the hell up!" the bloke said with a curled lip. He was roughly five foot five inches and was a wrecking ball of a man with dingy brown hair. He stood with a wide stance, his arms on his hips. He was dressed in black cargo pants and a long-sleeved black shirt. His gun was missing from the holster.

Teddy twisted to a sitting position. He winced, grabbing his skull, and peered at his left thigh. "Seriously? Duct tape," he said.

"Yeah, it's half-assed. We weren't ready for you to die and needed to stop the bleeding," the man said.

Teddy continued his assessment and peered around the room. He guesstimated it to be about thirteen feet by fifteen. Soundproof panels lined the walls, and the only window was a one-way mirrored glass.

"Who are you? Where am I?" Teddy slumped against the wall.

"You don't get to ask the questions," the guy said. "If it were up to me ... you'd be dead. No one shoots Bruno and lives to tell about it." He gestured his thumb to his shoulder.

Teddy peered at his handiwork. "You're lucky I'm injured, or you'd have more than a flesh wound, *Bruno*." Teddy sat tall.

Bruno turned his head away and returned to Teddy with a swift sucker punch to his solar plexus.

"Ooof." Teddy's air temporarily left his body, and he fell forward on his hands and knees. It was then he spotted an old dentist's chair with arm and leg straps. Beyond the chair were five plastic water filled jugs and a large wet rag. Here we go again, he thought.

Bruno repeatedly kicked Teddy until he was in a fetal position, his face flush against the icy floor.

"That's enough, Mr. Brown," a deep voice boomed through an intercom. "We need him alive for now. Leave the interrogations to me."

"Ah geez, Angus, you're takin' the fun out of it," Bruno said.

A few moments later, a six-foot six giant entered the room. He wore a black ski mask and was dressed in black from head to toe, including his plastic apron. The ogre's snug fitting t-shirt barely held in his bulging biceps. He had a black heart tattoo on his left arm.

"Never use my name," he said.

"Uh ... yeah, yeah sorry, Black Heart," Bruno said.

"Now, get my tools," Black Heart ordered.

Bruno rushed out of the room.

Black Heart bent down and snatched Teddy by his jacket collar and plopped him on the chair, strapping him in.

Teddy was too weak to fight and went limp like a rag doll.

Bruno returned moments later with a wheeled metal tray that contained pruning shears, a branch saw, scalpels, pliers of different sizes, zip ties, duct tape, a pre-filled syringe, and a cattle prod.

"We start slow, Bruno, and work our way up." The giant motioned to the tray.

"Bummer." Bruno snickered.

"Chena's orders," Black Heart said.

"Who the hell are you people?" Teddy gurgled breathlessly.

"Black Heart here is a pro at *enhanced interrogation techniques*." Bruno stood tall and pulled on his shirt.

"You mean torture," Teddy said.

"Eh, tomato, tomahto," Bruno said as he threw his hands out.

Black Heart took the pre-filled syringe off the tray and returned his attention to Teddy.

Teddy saw it coming, but he had nowhere to go. He reared his head and clenched his jaws as the needle pierced his neck. Moments later, his eyes were heavy. He assumed it was from the sodium pentothal coursing through his body. Teddy knew how to fight the urge. The famed truth serum was rarely effective on him.

"While we're waiting for it to work, show him the picture," a female's voice said over the intercom.

"It'll be my pleasure, Ms. Fin," Bruno said with a smirk as he took the cell from his side pocket.

Teddy bobbled his head as he studied the photo. He chortled and returned his gaze to the photograph of the dead woman.

Teddy watched as Bruno looked at the one-way glass and shrugged. Teddy let out another roar.

"How much of that shit did you give him, Black Heart?" Bruno asked.

"The usual dose, but I added a little extra something," Black Heart said.

Teddy let out a bark of laughter again.

"And what's so funny, Teddy *Reagan*." Bruno was inches from his face.

"Thas not my daughter," Teddy said with a slur.

"What?" Bruno peered closer to the picture. "It has to be."

Teddy smiled as if he had too many drinks and raised his brow. "My daughter has no tattoosh."

Just then, the intercom depressed, followed by a heavy sigh and a second of silence. "*What* is he talking about? You got the wrong woman?!" the lady said. "Bruno, are you sure you went AWOL in the army, or did they discharge you for being *incompetent*?"

"I swear, Ms. Fin. I, uh ... hired the best guys from the Bay Area. They even made it look like a robbery gone bad. And these guys never miss their target." Bruno studied the picture with furrowed, bushy brows. "Don't worry, don't worry," he said. "Bruno always has a Plan B." He stuffed the phone in his pocket and spun toward the one-way mirrored glass. "She has to go home sometime. She'll be dead before noon." He snickered.

"Ha, you can't touch my little girl. I molded her." He spat on Bruno.

Teddy watched as Bruno danced his fingers in the air over the torture devices. "Hey Black Heart, may I?"

"Eh, why not? Go for it." Black Heart stepped away with his arms crossed. "But don't touch the others. Those are mine."

Teddy braced himself. He was no stranger to cattle prods.

Bruno turned his attention to Teddy. "I bet she's never gone up against the cartel. And if we can get to you, imagine how easy it'll be to get to the rest of your family." He pressed the prongs into his skin and gave him a zap.

"Arrgh!"

"Scream as loud as you want. Ain't no one gonna hear you." Bruno jolted Teddy again. Teddy arched his back and dug his fingers into the chair, screaming. He felt every electric jolt sear through him.

Teddy was determined to be strong for his family. It was the least he could do.

CHAPTER 7

"**E**asy, Rose," Copper said, turning her gaze to me. "I promise, we're on ya side."

The driver of the Denali, a female with black curly hair rolled into a puffy bun, remained silent. She sucked her teeth and tilted her head, staring straight ahead as she gripped the wheel.

"Who are you ... really? And who do you work for?" I repositioned my body and peeked inside to make sure no one hid in the back seat. "Keep your hands where I can see them. I know you're both armed. I see the bulges in your sweatshirts," I said.

"We are not the enemy." The driver spoke her first words. "Now, holster your gun," she said in a low growl as she slowly turned her head.

S.S. DUSKEY

"Chill, Mia," Copper said. "Rose, I told you, a friend of your grandmother sent us. Now, can we put our freakin' hands down?" She watched as a car crept by, the driver ogling us. "You're drawing attention."

I shrugged. "Meh, it's my nosy neighbor. He and the others are used to me. They know what I do for a living," I said, waving at Gilbert Heart with my left hand, while I lowered my weapon with my right. "They kinda like me taking care of suspicious looking people in their hood." I conducted a mini threat assessment. Since neither gal reached for their guns, I re-holstered my Hellcat in my fanny pack, keeping my eyes trained on them.

"Just verify our story with your grandmother," Copper said.

"I tried, but she is *not* available at the moment," I said.

Although Copper's earlier story checked out with my grandmother, I remained vigilant after my hellish morning. "Now who is this *friend* of my grandmother ... and how did you know I'd come home? You didn't ping my burner, did you?" I leaned into the car's window.

Copper glanced at my waist and smirked. "Nice pack. Isn't it a bit 80s?"

"It's making a comeback. Anyway, answer my questions."

Copper sighed. "I was informed ya never do as you're told, are pretty damn stubborn, and don't ask for help. I know your lone wolf type. And no, I don't even have your burner number," she said.

"Yeah, yeah, so I've been told. You have to gain my trust. Now, who is this *friend*?"

"I think you've met him. His name is T—"

Just then, my Lexus RX 350 drove by. It was an upgrade since a crazed woman blew up my Highlander a few months ago. I followed with my eyes. And then I remembered I'd loaned it to my old boss, and now buddy, Amy Puckett. Amy's car was in the shop and her mechanic/boyfriend was picking her up at my house.

I lowered my shoulders and watched as Amy parked in my driveway and strolled to my front door.

"Be right back." I marched toward the house. "Hey ... Amy. Over here!" I shouted and waved.

Amy turned to me, smiled, and waved back. "H—" The moment she stepped on the doormat, BOOM! Amy's greeting disappeared in a high velocity blast. It was a scene from a war movie. Only it was real. An intense explosion shattered my home, and the earth shook under my feet. The blast wave knocked me down.

"Nooo!" I lay on the ground with my hands over my head as fragments of my tan and brown ranch-style home sailed through the air, plummeting to the ground and hammering my vehicle. "Amy ... no, no, no!" I bellowed again as I raised my arm to her. I looked over my shoulder and watched Copper. She appeared to be running in slow motion toward me. Her lips were moving and arms flailing, but I could not escape the ringing in my brain. All I saw were the whites of Copper's eyes as she drew closer. She was over me, yanking me to my feet.

Mia was immediately behind her, sliding to an abrupt stop. They dragged me to the Denali. Copper flung the rear passenger driver's side door open, shoved me in, and jumped into the front.

As we sped away, I twisted in my seat and gazed out the back window. I was in a trance as I watched my house go up in a blazing inferno. The neighbors bolted from their homes, with cell phones in hands. Some filmed, while, I hoped, others dialed 911. It wasn't the first time an explosion meant for me interrupted their tranquil neighborhood. But I hoped it would be the last.

CHAPTER 8

At first, I didn't notice my crimson-soaked sweatshirt. All I knew was Sue and Amy were both dead ... because of me. What had I done?

The buzzing in my brain continued, and I only caught part of Copper's and Mia's conversation.

Copper turned to me. "What do you thi—ah, crap. Hang on Rose," she said.

I peered down and saw blood everywhere. I pulled my sleeve back and discovered an oozing hole in my left forearm. I knew enough first aid to apply pressure. Just as I looked around for something, anything, Mia tossed me a blue bandana. I wrapped it around my arm and winced. I was queasy and the back seat spun.

I listened as Copper dialed. "Are you home?"

she asked. "I need a huge favor. A new friend had a piece of her home shred through her arm." She looked at me. "No, she's awake. It looks like it went completely through ... okay. Hey, O'Brien," she yelled back to me, "are you current on your tetanus?"

"Mm hm, with my track record I'd better be ... arrgh," I said with a pained moan.

"Did you copy? Thanks ... we'll be there in twenty." She disconnected.

"Fifteen," Mia said, flooring it.

"We have a friend who served with us. She's an ER physician's assistant at the local hospital," Copper calmly said.

"No hospitals!" I said.

"We're not. We're going to Nevada City," Mia said.

The fifteen-minute drive felt like an hour. But we finally arrived at 8:45 a.m. As we exited the SUV, a tall, thin brunette greeted us at the threshold of a modest ranch-style cabin. She wore medical scrubs with puppies on them and matching crocs. She met my height and weight.

"This is Butterfly." Copper introduced me to her.

"Butterfly?" I grimaced as I entered.

"The less you know, the better," Copper replied.

I watched Butterfly roll her eyes. "My name is Olive, but they call me Butterfly. Come in." She directed me to her kitchen. Butterfly turned her cement countertop into a make-shift trauma room. She equipped it with a suture and burn kit, gauze, bandages, tourniquets, quick clot, antiseptic spray, and a few other items I'd never seen.

Butterfly lived in a small two-bedroom, one bath log cabin, with open beams. Her place was cozy and hidden in the woods. It sat back on two acres. I didn't see the rest of the house, since I wasn't in the mood for a tour.

Mia pulled out a high back swivel bar stool for me. It was the first time I saw her face. She was Native American with beautiful smooth, olive skin. Her soft brown eyes crinkled when she smiled. Mia was in her mid-thirties and stood Saki's height, around five feet, five inches. She had a three-inch scar on her left cheek. And when she removed her sweatshirt, she was sleeved in tattoos.

I returned a tight smile and nodded to Mia. I refused to yield to the excruciating pain and grinned and bared it.

All three women had tough exteriors. But one thing was certain, they took care of their own. No questions asked.

Twenty minutes and five stitches later, I was bandaged and ready to rumble. Butterfly gave me antibiotics and extra strength Tylenol. She offered me a stronger drug, but I declined.

During the outpatient procedure, I gave Butterfly the condensed version of my crappy morning.

"So ... um yeah. I have no clothes, no home. I don't know who's trying to kill me or why." I exhaled an exaggerated sigh. I looked over to Mia and Copper, both sprawled out on the floor.

"To answer your question, cartel," Copper said matter-of-factly. "And the explosion was detonated by a pressure plate. It was placed under your doormat that was wired to an explosive device."

"Like an IED?" I asked.

"Mm hm, exactly," Mia responded.

"But why? Unless … it has something to do with Teddy!" I seethed.

CHAPTER 9

"Oh. Now you want to speak to me. I don't like being ignored," Chena barked.

"It was an important business meeting, not that it's any concern to you." Max watched the helicopter land on his helipad. "Are you on board?" he asked.

"No, I'm in the states waiting for SJ to arrive today. And you are coming with him. That's his chopper. Pack an overnight bag," she ordered.

"Excuse me? No one tells me what to do ... on *my* yacht." Max put his fists to his hips. "That wasn't part of our deal. You broke me out of prison to help find the Ghost, and that's exactly what I did. Now this is where you all thank me and leave me the *hell* alone." Max smirked, as if Chena could see his facial expression.

"Yes ... six months ago, when you sailed off into international waters. Not to mention millions of dollars later, no thanks to your blunder in Montana. Max, you had the Falcon and let it slip between your fingers." Chena exhaled a loud whoosh and lowered her voice. "Besides, *he* insists and wants a word with you."

"Who is SJ? And why do I care? I thought buyer and seller were never to meet. What happened to all the secrecy?"

"This goes way beyond our art deals."

Max watched two men carrying rifles exit the chopper. "You sent the goon squad. Is this really necessary?"

"Yes, they were on standby at one of SJ's villas in Mazatlán."

"I'm a fugitive and have warrants a mile long. Or don't you remember? I can't return to the states."

"That's something you and SJ have in common. You will both be flying under the radar with fake passports."

"Not again. I'm not changing my name," Max said.

"Not necessary. You won't be here long."

"What do you mean?"

"Never mind, I have to go. SJ is on the other line. And unlike you, I answer." Click. Chena disconnected.

The hair on the nape of his neck stood on end, and Max's stomach tightened as he stared down the barrel of an AK-47.

CHAPTER 10

Before James's mother passed away four months ago, she insisted he and Saki raise their child in the family home. James, being the only heir, obliged her request. But the taxes alone were more than James could afford with the FBI, so his mother left enough money to help offset Uncle Sam.

The home was originally built in the 1950s and was located on Palm Island, an exclusive eighty-two-acre man-made island in Biscayne Bay. The estate was in the Hart family trust, his mother's surname. James preferred it that way—safe and under the radar, or so he'd thought. The 2,500 square foot, four bedroom, three and a half bath, multimillion-dollar estate set on a quarter acre with a private boat dock was minutes from Miami.

The normal fifty-minute drive from Fort Lauderdale to Palm Island took closer to an hour and a half. James took I-95 South to 395, taking frequent exits and returning to the main highway.

"Babe, why is it taking so long? I have to pee. The baby is sitting on my bladder." Saki wiggled in her seat.

"Sorry, Sak. I thought we had someone following us, but after the last U-turn, it was a false alarm." James peered in the rearview mirror.

James's radio chirped. "We are in position, JP."

"Copy," James replied.

Saki looked at him with furrowed brows.

"I have some agents on the house, and a couple of my SWAT team members are going to follow us in until we get to the bottom of this."

They pulled up to the Palm Island security gate. James showed his badge and government issued ID. "We are not expecting any visitors, except the family members you have listed and my team."

The armed guard opened the gates.

Just as they cleared security, Saki's phone buzzed with an alert. She'd forgotten about her app from her old stomping ground. She gasped and held her hand to her mouth. "No, no, no!"

"What? What is it?" James asked.

Saki handed James the phone.

BREAKING NEWS: An early morning explosion on the three hundred block of Oak Road in Grass Valley took the life of an unidentified female. The victim is presumed to be the homeowner. Her identity has not been confirmed, pending positive identification and family notification. Nearby residents have been evacuated and are still not cleared to return to their homes. Stay tuned for the latest update ...

Saki pointed to the picture. "That's Rose's home. Th ... that's why we can't get a hold of her," Saki said with a heavy sob.

James looked wide-eyed at Saki. "No, no, no. This isn't real ... it can't be. I'm gonna make a call." James's voice shook as he returned the phone to his wife and used his own. "Crap, still same voice mail. I'm going to call Kevin."

Just then, Saki's phone buzzed with a text. She read it and grabbed James's hand. "Roses are in bloom." Saki lowered her shoulders and threw her head against the headrest. "That would've been nice to see *before* that news report!" she said with a scrunched nose. "These damn family cryptic messages." She caressed her belly. "Sorry, baby, Mommy gets a free pass on that one."

"See, I told you, Rose is okay. But we've got to act as if it's real." James grabbed Saki's hand and kissed it.

"I don't need to act ... it *is* real. Her house is gone! I can't imagine what she is going through. She's always been there for me." Saki clutched her cell. "And I ... I can't even contact her."

"I know. I don't like this one bit. But I'm not leaving you alone and besides, you are too far along," James said.

"Trust me, I'd go myself if I could," she said. "But you can … and she needs you. I'll be safe. I have extra protection. And Gretel, your new FBI Investigative Specialist will be here soon to install the security system." Saki wiped her eyes. "Daisy said she was a whiz with surveillance equipment."

James's phone buzzed with an incoming text. "Crap … mandatory training. Babe, I have to. This SWAT gig is no joke. And you are correct. We have the best here." He gazed at the house.

Saki turned to James. "After training … please go! I'm sure Uncle Tubbs can fly you out there. Kaylee will arrive shortly, and Heidi is returning this afternoon from her Bahamas trip. We can all finish the baby's room. You know, fun girl stuff," she said, as she flashed her husband a toothy smile and batted her eyelashes. "We'll have plenty of folks. Look, if I'm not safe at the home of an *elite* FBI SWAT team member's house, I'm not safe anywhere." Saki beamed with pride at her husband. "Now unlock the door before I wet myself."

CHAPTER 11

My burner rang and smoke billowed from my ears. I knew who it was.

"Your son is something else ... but you already know that. Two friends murdered ... before noon and my house goes up like a freakin' roman candle, not to mention a piece of my home punctured my arm, and don't get me started on my Lexus. But more importantly ... my friends are *dead* ... boy, when I get my hands on him," I barked without coming up for air.

Silence fell on the line.

"Grandma Lil ... are you there?"

"You done?" she asked in a firm tone.

"Yeah," I said, letting out a heavy sigh. "I'm ... I'm, I don't know what I am." My bottom lip quivered, and I sucked in a suffocated sniffle.

"You've got every right to feel that way. And I am truly sorry about your friends. It's not easy ... and I have more bad news," Grandma said. "But first you need to flush the anger and resentment toward your father."

"Will you *please* tell me what's going on? I don't do well when I'm not in the driver's seat."

"Right now, it's not only about you. The gals have an encrypted laptop."

Copper had walked outside during my rant and retrieved the computer from her vehicle. She set it on the countertop in front of me.

I flipped it open.

"The passcode is 'Violet1985#,'" Grandma said.

My heart softened at the mention of my mother's name again. "Grandma, you sound as if you are in a tunnel?"

"We are ... sort of."

"You're no longer in your com center in Darby?" I put the phone on speaker and set it down as I entered the passcode.

"I'm further back. It wasn't necessary to show you everything while you were here. There was too much going on. We'll discuss that later. We may have a bug and are taking every safety measure. We've had to shut down our systems and are going black and using archaic stone-aged equipment ... did the video come through?"

I played it and a painful jab pierced my heart.

"This happened on Sunday," Grandma said.

"Why did you wait two days to show me?"

"He's been dark. The video wasn't unscrambled until a few hours ago. And I needed to get you to safety first. It was also a good thing your father has ADS-B."

"What's that?"

"Automatic Dependent Surveillance-Broadcast. To make it simple, it's a tracking system using data from the plane's navigation system. I have a flight tracking app. No doubt the people who took him have the same app. All you need is the plane's tail number. Another Big Brother move."

"Wait … how did you find me? Do you have a tracker on me too?" I furrowed my brows.

"Have you forgotten what I did for a living? I have connections all over the globe," she said. "And yes, I've had eyes on you since Max escaped from prison."

"For six months, Grandma?" I shook my head, rubbing the bandage on my arm.

"Yes … I won't apologize. Anyway, with you in Napa, my Sacramento people were too far away, and Copper and Mia just finished a special op in the Bay Area, so they were available."

"Special operation?" I shot glances at the two of them.

Copper's and Mia's eyes were closed. They were undoubtedly wiped out from their early morning assignment. It was then that I glimpsed Copper's prosthetic right leg. Hence her limp. I shook my head and returned to the conversation.

"The less you know, the better," Grandma

replied.

"Mm hm." I pursed my lips and nodded as if she could see me. "So ... do you think he's alive?" My voice softened again.

By this time, our gracious hostess had brought out granola, yogurt, muffins, and coffee for her weary friends. I mouthed a *thank you* to Butterfly as the aroma from the java wafted in the air, reviving me.

"I believe so or they wouldn't have come after you. You must go to the crash site to see if he left anything. I just texted you and Copper the plane's last known coordinates. Your father must've had engine problems right after takeoff from Tiger Field in Fernley. I have a friend with the NTSB. They didn't receive word of a crash or a Mayday call. But one thing is certain, *if* he's alive, they're working him. They are using his family as a means of negotiation. They already think you are dead ..." Her voice trailed off.

"I'm sorry, Grandma. I was only thinking of myself," I said.

"Rosie. Life is too precious and short to hold on to resentment. A lesson you can learn."

I went silent for a spell, avoiding the topic. "I'll cruise out to the site. I can handle it. Besides, these gals can use some re—"

The ladies' eyes popped open, and they sat upright at my comment.

All three let out a collective sigh and yelled, "No," in unison.

"You are just like your father! Don't you dare go solo, Granddaughter. You don't have that kind of training yet. And you don't really wear an 'S' on your chest. These people are far too dangerous."

"Okay, okay, I get it. Did Teddy have the Falcon? I know he was retrieving the rest of the ..." I glanced at the ladies and cleared my throat, "information."

"Yes. But he was using a different medium to relay it. He didn't say what it was. This was going to be his final job," she said. "We should be back online shortly once we are cleaned. Since we'll be dark, I'll contact you. Also ... you *need* to follow the protocol. You ignored it when you went home and were careless. I set it in place for the family's protection." Grandma lectured me like I was a child.

"I'm sorry Gran. It won't happen again ... wait a minute. Copper and Mia were waiting for me at home. You knew I'd go there first."

"Yes, I did ... because that's what I would've done." She chuckled.

"I promise to follow it this time." I let out a heavy sigh. "Gran, where do you think they took him?"

"I have my people working on his location. My hunch is, he's not far. But once they discover you're alive, Satan will summon his imps. Keep a low profile."

"Copy ... but what about the family? They need to know I'm okay."

"Lily handled it and by now James has taken every precaution with Saki and Kayl—" Silence fell on the line.

"Grandma? Lillian?" Just like that, she cut

out.

I dropped my head on the counter and rubbed my face. "Could this day get any worse?"

CHAPTER 12

Max narrowed his eyes, clinging to his lightweight navy Gucci jacket as the armed thug shoved him to the rear of the Cessna Citation. He spun. "It's bad enough you watched me pack and threw me into the chopper like a savage animal. But so help you, if you touch me one more time," Max said as he was nose to nose with the hooligan.

Just then, the goon's phone rang. "Hola ... for you," he said with broken English as he handed Max the cell.

"Yes," Max answered curtly as he held the thug's gaze.

"Maxwell, darling. I see you made it to SJ's plane."

"*This* is SJ's?" He peered around. "Humpf, disappointing."

"What don't you understand about flying *under* the radar?"

"Chena, why can't SJ and I discuss business here in Mexico? Why the states?"

"SJ has personal reasons, and it's not for me to inquire. Anyway … I take it you have your computer?" Chena asked.

Max let out a heavy sigh. "Yes."

"Good. Give Manny his cell and answer yours when I call. And turn on your laptop. I'm linking a live feed."

He threw the phone to Manny, plopped in the rear seat of the plane, and opened his computer. A few moments later, his cell rang. "What kind of game are you playing?" Max asked through gritted teeth.

"I know you're used to being in charge, but we all have to answer to someone. Now … for your pre-flight entertainment."

He set the phone on the seat next to him and put it on speaker. Max gaped at the video.

A familiar, blond-haired man shouted. He sat on an old dentist's chair. His hands were secured to the arms of the chair and his legs were bound. Two men stood on either side. One was short, the other had a much larger build and wore a ski mask. The masked guy picked up a pair of pliers from a tray and twisted the man's fingers. Blood curdling shouts rang out again.

They appeared to be in a basement. There were gray soundproof panels on three sides. The fourth wall was a one-way mirrored glass. Max had a similar room in his Key West home.

"Let me get you up to speed, Max," Chena said. "The masked man's name is Black Heart, the shorter is Bruno. If you recall, I sent Bruno to aid in your escape from custody. And I believe you are already acquainted with the Ghost."

Max swallowed hard. The last time he saw the Ghost, a.k.a. Teddy Reagan, he was eleven. Teddy and Max's father were partners in a series of thriving art galleries in Southern Florida. Their families would meet at his parents' home in Key West, where they had weekly business meetings.

He remembered it like it was yesterday. Max was playing with his best pal, Rose, downstairs when a shot rang out from the boatshed. The fatal gunshot changed *all* their lives forever. Max stared at the man who took his childhood away. But why wasn't he pleased with the show?

"Aww ... the big wig fuckin' art snitch. You're not so tough now, are you?" Bruno said with a wide stance as he shook his hand. "You made me cut my hand on your face." He wiped his knuckle on his pant leg.

Max sunk with his arms crossed.

"Do it again, Black Heart," Bruno said.

Teddy let out another torturous scream.

"You wanna know why we call Angus 'Black Heart'?" Bruno asked.

Teddy moaned.

"Well, I'll tell you. Because his heart's black and he ain't got no soul. He could do this all day." Bruno smiled widely with his under bite at the CCTV. He turned to Teddy. "So ... are ya ready to give us the info?"

"I ... told you, don't have it ... destroyed in the plane crash ... you caused." Teddy said breathlessly as he spit blood in Bruno's direction.

Chena zoomed into Teddy's face. He was almost unrecognizable. His lips were cracked and bleeding, his eyes swollen, and his clothing torn to shreds.

Max shook his head and bit his lip.

"Max," Chena said. "Why so quiet? I'd thought you'd enjoy this. I mean, didn't this man kill your father?"

Max felt his face redden as he listened to the screams coming from the computer. While Max was no stranger to Draconian torture measures, he could not watch it anymore. He flipped the computer screen down and gazed out the window. A year ago, Max would've eagerly watched with Chena, but he no longer enjoyed the macabre theatrics. He wanted to be a better man, for Rose. Even if it meant not reveling in the torture and ultimate death of the person who he held responsible for taking his childhood.

"Max, are you still watching? I have a couple of other things to show you," Chena said.

Max cleared his throat. "It's unnecessary. I'm bored with this ... and why are we still sitting at the airport?"

"Aww, Maxie, you're taking the fun out of this for me." Chena sighed. "And to answer your question SJ should be arriv—"

Just then, the plane's door opened. A man climbed on board. He stood five feet, ten inches with a dark mustache and goatee. Not even a dash of gray. Most likely dyed. He wore a tan, bespoke, lightweight cotton suit, beige straw fedora, and sunglasses. He removed his hat and glasses and flashed a cheeky grin.

"Hello, old friend," he said with a Spanish accent. He wore his black hair slicked back, and his hazel eyes were dark, harder than Max remembered.

Max's palms were moist and sweat dripped down his forehead. *"Stanley James Albrecht-Cordova,"* he said.

CHAPTER 13

It was eleven in the morning, two friends murdered, my house gone, and I had five stitches. Not how I'd planned the day. By now, my tummy would be full, and I'd be sitting in a boring class, waiting for the day to end. Sue would be sending me pictures of our crazy night out. Instead, I had a throbbing arm, and I was being driven to a crash site by two women I'd never met.

I tossed my head back and closed my eyes as the sun's rays warmed me through the window. I drifted through the heavens. My husband, Bradley, hovered over one cloud and my mother on another. They died three months apart, so it was fitting they were together, laughing and smiling in the afterlife. I floated to them, reaching out. How I yearned for their touch. But they didn't see me, as if I wasn't there. Did they miss me? Or even think about me? As I glided away, I heard a faint, melodic whisper that sounded like my mother's voice. *Do not let your heart be troubled, and do not be afraid.*

I jolted awake to the SUV, jarring. We'd just turned off NV 439 headed south to Silver Springs. Peace fell over me for a moment at my mother's soothing voice, quoting John 14:27. "Do not be afraid, Rose," I mumbled.

As I sat straight, pain shot through my body. The time on my phone read 11:40 a.m., so I popped more Tylenol, took a bite of a chalky power bar Butterfly gave me, and washed it down with water.

After six miles, Mia yanked the wheel and took a sharp left onto a bumpy, dirt road, right after a power plant. We fishtailed. I grabbed the "Oh Shit" handle. "Crap, wrong arm," I said with a wince.

"Sorry ladies, it came up faster than I thought," Mia said.

"All good," I replied with a grimace.

We approached power poles and a closed cattle gate with a posted *No Trespassing* sign. Mia stopped sharply. Copper popped out, opened the gates, and we made our way through.

"According to the coordinates, the plane should be to the east. It may be in the canyon off here," Copper read from her GPS.

Ten minutes into the rough and tumble terrain, I spotted the plane in the distance.

"There it is!" I shouted and pointed.

Another five minutes and the three of us jumped out.

"How could anyone survive this?" I muttered to myself as I inspected the area around the charred plane's remains. Copper and Mia fanned out and did a grid search.

"Here's the rock outcropping from the video." Copper pointed.

We trekked over and that's when I spied the watch with the pictures along with his smashed phone. Tears welled as I scanned the surrounding area, looking for anything useful. I wiped my eyes and inspected the watch. It had a black leather band with a plastic case covered by a stainless-steel mask with a brushed silver finish and glass. The face was cracked, and the time stopped precisely at twelve o'clock. The irony. I was unsure of its significance, but it belonged to Teddy and was the only thing left. So, I slapped it on my wrist and stuffed the pictures in my pack.

"It looks like a dead end." Mia put her hand out to me. "Sorry, Rose. I didn't mean de—"

"No worries." I tried to give her my best *no apology needed* look.

We walked back to the SUV in defeated silence. As soon as we hit NV 439 North, I broke the stillness. "I feel like we missed something."

Copper turned to me. "We scoured every bit. The only thing left were the pictures and watch, everything else was destroyed."

"True." I puffed my cheeks. "Hey, as much

fun as I've had with you ladies, I need my own wheels," I said.

Copper grinned at me. "You and your grandma are on the same page. She rented a vehicle for you. It's at the Truckee-Tahoe Airport, she knows a gu—"

Whop, whop, whop, whop.

Our SUV vibrated. Out of nowhere, a helicopter's landing skid was in our field of vision, buzzing the Yukon like a falcon swooping on a rabbit.

CHAPTER 14

Teddy's hair was drenched in his sweat and the salty taste of blood lingered in his mouth from where Bruno punched him. He gaped through the slits in his engorged eyes as he watched Black Heart change torture devices. Suddenly, the door flung wide, and a woman stepped inside. Teddy assumed she was the voice from the intercom. She was in her mid-forties, and an Alaska Native American with long, black, silky hair with streaks of silver and dark brown eyes. She stood five eleven with a confident and lean build. She wore loafers with a white, fitted pants suit.

She held her hand to Black Heart. "That'll be all for now," she said, stoned faced.

"Yes, Ms. Fin." Black Heart stepped back.

"It's Chena," she said, staring at her captive.

"Teddy Reagan. We meet face to face. I've heard so much about you. Do you know who I am?"

Teddy did not say anything and bobbled his head. He followed Chena with his eyes.

"I guess it's not who *I* am, but who my employers are. You see, they're not as patient as I've been." She moved over to the tray and visually inspected the bloody tools with her hands clasped behind her. "It appears you have been a thorn in everyone's side. Your reign of terror is coming to an end," she said.

"I already told Jethro and the little fella," Teddy said, "the information was destroyed in the plane crash. So, there's nothing to tell. The feds don't have it. I swear."

"Do you swear on your family's life?" Chena pursed her lips. "Perhaps you need a reminder of what we are capable of doing." She turned to Bruno and snapped her fingers. "Laptop," she said.

Bruno left the room and returned moments later. He placed the computer on the tray and opened it. Chena scrolled through and produced it to Teddy.

He leaned in and through blurred vision read the breaking news out of Grass Valley. "She did nothing to you," Teddy shouted as tears welled in his eyes. He felt as if his heart was ripped out of his chest and crushed to pieces. He lowered his head in shame. His eldest daughter, murdered because of him. His little Rose Bud.

"Now, do you take me seriously?" Chena

closed the screen and towered over Teddy and glared. "Where is the information?" she asked slowly and deliberately through gnashed teeth.

"Why should I tell you, you're gonna kill me. And you've already killed my daughter." He returned a snarl.

She stood tall and pressed her suit. She sauntered behind Teddy and bent down and hissed in his ear. "Yes. Yes, we did. But you have two more." She slithered to the front of the room and gazed at her reflection in the glass, smoothing her brows. "One is expecting a baby, and the other is a resident in Jacksonville. What a proud father you must be."

"You people are *monsters*! Leave them alone," he shouted.

"Yeah ... no can do." She spun. "Where is the information?!"

"It was destroyed in the plane crash. I told you. The wreck you caused. It's your fault. And how did you know I wouldn't die too?"

"Contaminated fuel? Please, you're a top-notch pilot. We knew you'd be able to handle the landing." Chena threw a hand to the window.

The hooded titan presented another pre-filled syringe in hand. "This is a new drug. It will work or kill him. Either way, it's worth trying," Black Heart said, approaching Teddy.

Teddy pulled away, but his attempt was futile.

CHAPTER 15

"**B**ird approaching!" Mia shouted. "What are these assholes doing?" She peered through the windshield and up, looking for the chopper.

The helicopter's rotor downwash pounded the Denali. Mia slammed on her brakes and performed a reverse 180 or J-turn as it's referred to in tactical driver training. If we weren't running from a whirly bird looking to peck our eyes out, I would've enjoyed the maneuver.

The Bell 206 followed suit and fired on us, turning the hood of the Denali into Swiss Cheese.

Copper turned to me. "Long guns behind you, hurry," she shouted as she pulled her Glock 9 from her holster, leaned out the window, and shot back at the hovering chopper.

I hurriedly unbuckled and turned. My heart pounded through my ears. While I was ass over the backseat, Mia was playing dodgeball with the helicopter. She swerved to the right, hit dirt, and fishtailed onto the main road. I pinged around like a pinball but managed to grab an MK18 from the packed cargo compartment, handed it to Copper.

Just as I had the second one in my hand, I looked out the rear window and was nose to nose with the great white. In my case it was orange. Two men hung from either side taking aim at us. I ducked and sheltered my face. The back window shattered. I should have thanked them, as it gave me a perfectly unobstructed line. I returned fire, hitting both the pilot and the guy right behind her.

They returned rapid fire, blowing out both rear tires, causing the Denali to spin wildly. This time, Mia could not regain control. We slammed against the guardrail and flew over barbed wire. The vehicle came to an abrupt stop headfirst into a dirt mound. The front air bags deployed, and dust filled the vehicle. All was quiet for a millisecond except for the incessant buzzing in my ears. After today, a hearing test was on my to do list. If I survived.

I landed on the floorboard and held my breath, waiting for the chopper to return, but it didn't. I assessed my body. No new dents, but my stitches were oozing. As luck would have it, a green military blanket from the back made its way over the seat and shielded me from the flying rubble.

I eased to a sitting position when a burning stench filled the Yukon and smoke billowed from the engine.

"Shit. We gotta get out!" Copper shouted as she pushed out her door.

I yanked on my door handle. It would not open. I tried the other side, same thing. Copper wrenched from the outside, but her attempts were also futile. I furiously kicked at the closed windows. It didn't work. "Don't panic, Rose." I reassured myself. I started for the rear window, but it was inaccessible with all the equipment crammed in the back. Since I had no time to toss the gear out, I scanned the interior and spotted the MK. I snatched the weapon and busted out the rear passenger window. I used the blanket and placed it over the shattered glass and slithered out.

Copper and I ran to the driver's side and banged on the window. Mia was not moving and unresponsive.

"Mia!" Copper and I shouted simultaneously.

I called out again as I flung the door wide. "Crap. She's got a head wound." I pressed on the seat belt release, but it was jammed. Copper bolted to the rear of the vehicle to get her bag of tools when it occurred to me I had my Benchmade Infidel stiletto knife in my fanny pack. I grabbed it, slid the action button forward, and the blade automatically released. Just as I cut her free and retracted my blade, flames shot out from the engine.

We quickly scooped her from the burning SUV and gingerly laid her on the desert floor. A millisecond later, *whoosh*. The vehicle burst into a blazing inferno.

"I fine," Mia slurred as her eyelids fluttered and her head lolled to the side.

"Fine, my ass. You have a bump on your hard head and you're bleeding. Don't move," Copper said.

As Copper examined Mia for neck injuries, I yanked my burner cell from my side pocket and started to dial 911.

"Stop," Copper yelled. "These people are well connected. We can't trust anyone."

"But she needs he—"

In the distance, a black Cadillac Escalade with dark tinted windows approached from the north.

My stomach tightened. I removed my pistol from my pack and prepared for another gun battle.

CHAPTER 16

Max glared at the man. "It's been a long time, *Stanley James.*"

"I go by SJ now ... and yes, it has been, *Sammy.*" SJ made his way to the seat across from Max.

"It's Max," he said with a clenched jaw. "And I should've known you were behind all this." He waved his hand at the armed men.

"To say you disappointed me is an understatement. I thought I taught you better. You've gone soft and let that redhead cloud your judgment." SJ rolled his neck, cracking it. "But I hear she is no longer a problem. The rest of the family will be eliminated if the Ghost doesn't provide what I want," SJ said, staring through Max.

"Her family is of no concern to me." Max

raised his brow and shrugged.

"I've been watching your career at a distance since you were my protégé. And I felt like a proud father." SJ pounded his chest. "Until now. How can you let my personal information get in the clutches of the feds? What was the first thing I taught you when I picked you up from juvenile hall?"

"Are we going there with another lesson? I'm *not* a 17-year-old, pimply-faced virgin. I've made just as much money as you. And I have to say, I'm a better cleaner. Not some lowly drug dealer."

SJ slammed his fists on the seat.

Max jumped.

"How dare you speak to me in this manner. I am *not* a drug dealer." His accent was more Spanish than American. "I owed your father my life and promised him I'd look out for you. And this is how you repay me? No more!" SJ yelled.

Max contemplated for a spell and changed the subject. "Stan—uh, SJ, why *are* we going to the states? It's too risky … for both of us."

"I have personal reasons," SJ replied.

"Look." Max stood. "I don't need this or you. I held up my end of the bargain. I handed the Ghost over to you."

Manny was promptly on Max. He shoved him back in the seat with the rifle in his face.

Just then, the pilot turned. "We are ready for takeoff. Calexico first stop," he said, handing the men their new passports. "I have a man waiting at the port of entry to clear us. And then on to Truckee-Tahoe Airport."

SJ waved his armed goons off the plane and returned to Max. "You may have led me to the Ghost, but your job is not over. No, no, my friend. You are insurance for me."

Max glared. "We are not friends." He growled and slumped back with arms crossed.

CHAPTER 17

"Status?" Chena paced the living room of her boss's Incline Village mansion with her phone on speaker.

Silence fell on the line.

Chena furrowed her brows. "Well? The Ghost told us where to find it ... and did you?" she said with an eerie calmness.

"Not exactly. They beat us to it," a man with a gruff voice responded.

"What? Who?" Her voice went up an octave.

"By the time our chopper arrived, a vehicle was leaving the crash site."

"And?"

The fellow let out a heavy sigh. "We exchanged gunfire and two of my people were shot, including the pilot. One of them is dead. We barely made it to safety."

"You incompetent baboon." She sat tall on a cushioned seat on the windowsill, closed her eyes and drew a deep meditative breath. The heat from the sun shining through the window eased her for the moment.

"Seriously, lady? I lost a good man, and the pilot has a fuckin' bullet hole in her arm."

Chena popped her eyes opened. "*What* did you call me? Would you like to re-think that? Bruno may have found you. But I can make you disappear, and no one would know or even care."

The man did not respond.

"That's what I thought." Chena stood.

"Um ... there's something else. There were three women in the vehicle and ... I got a close look at one of 'em. I believe the target is still alive."

Chena let out an exaggerated moan. "The price on her head has doubled, dead *or* alive. And I want the information. Am I clear?!"

"Crystal."

"SJ will be landing in two hours. That's your deadline."

"Are you kidding? I'm gonna need more time ... and money."

"I just gave you twenty in bitcoins."

"The chopper is out of commission and I'm down two people," he yelled. "Now that I know she is still alive, I want her as bad as you ... maybe more."

"Your personal vendetta is of no consequence to me. I don't care how you get her, just do it."

"I've got another plan. There's chatter of a team being put together by my old army unit. A local op. You and I *know* what that's about. And they need another player. I am positive I'm in. I'll keep you posted."

"You better ... or else."

"Or else what? You gonna kill me? Come on lady, you don't scare me. A man without a family has nothing to lose. Ten more ... in cash." He disconnected.

Chena glared at the phone. No one spoke to Chena Fin in that manner.

Her cell rang again. She sighed. "Yes, Sir."

"Do you have things handled?"

"On track, SJ."

"It is a yes or no answer. Do you have the information?"

"Soon."

"Then you are not on track ... handle it." Click. The call ended.

Chena clenched her fists and chucked her phone across the room. She didn't have the nerve to tell SJ that Rose was still alive.

CHAPTER 18

"Stand down, Rose. He's a friendly." Copper eased her hand on mine.

I re-holstered and furrowed my brows. "How'd he find us so fast?" I asked.

"Our vehicles have tracking devices, and I sent a 911 alert on group text when the bird buzzed us."

I stared through her. "Who are you people?"

"Former special forces. That's all you need to know. Or want to know." Copper shook her head as the Escalade came to an abrupt stop. "Come on, help me with Mia," she said.

The driver popped out and flung the rear door wide.

Copper and I eased Mia in the back, behind the driver. "There's a first aid kit on the floorboard," she said, peering at my oozing arm.

The driver gave Copper a fist bump as he propped his glasses on top of his bald head. "Hey doll, ya look like shit," he said with a thick east coast accent, closing the door. The man met my height and had striking green eyes. He wore blue jeans, a black tactical fleece jacket, and same boots as the gals. He probably had a hard body at one point that turned into a marshmallow.

"So do you, Vino," she said, wincing as she angled in the front passenger seat, clutching her left leg.

I slid in next to Mia and studied Vino for a spell as he slipped behind the wheel. There was something oddly familiar to him. "Have we met?" I asked.

"Nah … I'd remember a hottie like you." He raised his brows and smiled at me in the rearview mirror as he kicked up rocks.

Now he *definitely* reminded me of someone. The resemblance was uncanny. I shook it off.

"My apologies," Copper said. "This is Vino. We served together. But his highness missed this morning's op." She gave him a playful slug in the arm. "He is one of seven we have for today."

"Eight. We found another dude," Vino said.

"We don't need another *dude*. Ya know I don't play well with outsiders." Copper turned to me. "No offense, O'Brien," she said.

I gave her a nod as I cleaned Mia's head wound.

"Well, Mia and you are now out of play."

Vino peered at her leg. "And you know the guy. He served one tour with us."

"Hey, my arms are still good." She flipped him off. "I can still shoot ... asshole. I got this," she said.

He laughed as he put on his black Ray Bans. "You love me, you want to kiss me." He playfully sang as he shimmied his shoulders.

"Seriously? For a dude, you've watched Miss Congeniality way too much," Copper said.

"Eh. What can I say ... gotta love me some Sandy B ... hunh," he said, grabbing his crotch.

"I think I just threw up in my mouth a little." I grimaced. "Yep. I did." As I closely examined Mia's head, I noticed an egg-sized bump forming, most likely a concussion. "And I didn't think my day was gonna get any crazier," I said under my breath.

"I'm just bustin' ya chops. I believe in levity. Life is too damn serious. And it's about to get more real. Like my mutha says, 'Hold on to your tutu.'" Vino laughed.

Mia mumbled and let out a pained moan.

"She needs a doctor," I said.

"No," everyone, including Mia, shouted simultaneously.

"Butterfly is on her way," Copper said.

"I feel like my brain's been rattled. I'll be fine once I get rid of this headache. Speaking of ... shut the hell up, Vino." She kicked his seat. "You ramble worse than an old bat," she said as she released her tight bun, rubbing her head as her thick hair draped down her shoulders and fell below her hips.

It was a good sign. I didn't want to be the cause of more deaths today. I expelled an exaggerated sigh as I applied antibacterial spray and re-bandaged my arm. I could've used that narcotic Butterfly offered, or better yet, a shot of whiskey.

CHAPTER 19

Chena pulled her Armani double-breasted jacket collar around her neck as she paced the dock. Springtime in Tahoe was unpredictable, and the wind had picked up. She supervised Bruno and Black Heart as they carted Teddy in a wheelbarrow down to the boathouse. His arms and legs dangled over the sides.

"Hey, boss. If SJ's mother is dying upstairs, why did he want us to bring this guy here?" Bruno asked.

"I don't know. But someone is coming to read her last rites today, so we need to keep Teddy quiet. We'll move him tonight after SJ gets here. We may have another body." She looked over her shoulder. "Hurry, the hospice workers are doing a shift change," she said.

Chena's phone rang. She marched to the house and stood in the backyard. "Status," Chena answered.

"I'm in. We meet tonight in Tahoe City."

"And you're certain they don't have a clue?" she asked.

"Trust me. I'll handle what your lackeys couldn't," said the man with the gruff voice.

"Just get me the data. You can do what you please with her. I sent you a picture."

"There isn't anything special about it," the man said.

"That's exactly the point." Chena's phone buzzed. She looked at her caller ID. "I've got to take this." She switched calls. "Status?"

"I'm sitting on the pregnant one right now. I got a bonus for you. The other sister arrived a few minutes ago. You know, the doctor. You can call off your men from up north."

"Perfect. It should be like stealing candy from a baby. When I give you the word, take them out."

"I am not okay with killing a pregnant woman and her unborn child. That is cult shit right there. I swear I will walk away from this operation right no—"

"Have you forgotten why we own you?" Chena calmly asked.

The woman did not respond.

"That's what I thought. If all goes well, you won't have to kill either woman."

"Oka—uh, I gotta go. Another agent just arrived. I have to get rid of him. I'll keep you posted."

"Don't blow this," Chena said, and disconnected. She ambled to the house, shook out of her coat, and went to the bar. She looked at her watch. "Noon, perfect time for a drink." She poured a whiskey, anticipating SJ's arrival.

CHAPTER 20

The time on the dash of my rented Rubicon Jeep read one thirty. Vino, Copper, and Mia took off to God knew where. They were tight-lipped. I was as well. Part of the Violet Protocol was not to tell a soul about the location of the safe house. When we departed, Copper advised me she would be in touch, and we would rendezvous later to meet the rest of the team.

Copper's last words to me were, "Keep a low profile." Like I didn't hear that from Grandma. But I blew that out the window when I came face to face with the enemy and shooting them was not lying low. By now, the bad guys knew I was above ground. Heavy sigh.

Since it was still radio silent on Grandma's end, I sent Lily a text. *Code 4, negative on info, en route to Violet's.* Short and sweet. Lily Cazier was my grandmother's right-hand assistant, my new BFF, and, after kidnapping Titos in Montana, my partner in crime.

The moment I exited the Truckee-Tahoe Airport, my stomach rumbled and my arm throbbed. The morning snack disappeared from my belly, and I had pills to take. Since I was dead, it didn't matter how I ate, right? Grease was the solution. It worked when I partied too hard in college.

Instead of going left on CA Hwy 267 to Lake Tahoe, I turned right toward Truckee. I drove through town looking for fast food and stopped at The Golden Arches. It was closest to Hwy 89 and a short drive to Homewood. If only all my decisions today were that easy.

I pulled up to the drive through and ordered a double D, minus the cheese. Although I was purportedly departed, I didn't want to be a chunky corpse. So, I added a Diet Coke with my fries and water. I got my food and backed into a parking spot and idled. I wolfed down my fries first since they are always best warm. I rolled my eyes in the back of my head and let out a gratifying sigh as the salty, crispy fries tasted like bits of heaven. Then I popped my pills.

Just as I had my watering mouth around the burger, the burner phone vibrated. I jumped. I needed to change it to a ring or chirp or some other melodious tune. I peered at the cell. Unknown caller. Hmm, few people had this number.

I hit answer and paused. "Speak," I barked.

"Woof? What the hell kind of greeting is that, Red?"

"Why do you insist on calling me 'Red', *Agent* O'Malley?"

"You sound good for a dead person. And seriously? The formality? And after all we've been through. You should be happy. I only have nicknames for people I like, and I don't like too many ... but you're one of my favs." He laughed.

"I'm flattered. But you didn't call me to talk about nicknames. So ... how's the FBI/CIA Joint Terrorism Task Force treating you?" Yes, I was the queen of avoiding topics I was uncomfortable with. It was obvious Kevin liked me and the feelings were mutual, but I was not ready to go there. It had only been a year since my beloved Bradley was murdered.

"I'm on a little vacay in South Lake Tahoe. I'm best man at my cousin's wedding. But I just got the craziest message from your brother-in-law." His tone changed. "What the hell is going on?" he said.

"How *did* you get this number?" I asked, skirting the question again. The few people in my drama llama world, the better.

"Your grandma. I had to practically threaten to get your burner number. You know, you're a walking crime scene these days," Kevin said with a sigh. "But seriously, I'm sorry about your friends and your house ..." His voice trailed away. "Are you okay? And where are you? James and your sister are worried."

My heart ached at not having any contact

with my baby sister. "I've been playing telephone tag with James," I said. "But they know I'm okay ... I'm fine. I have people helping me. I got this." I slurped my soda and shrugged, as if he could see me.

"Let me guess, Grandma connections? I'm a bit skeptical of her tactics. I had a hunch there was something the two of you were hiding at her house in Darby."

You mean someone. I could never tell James or Kevin that Lily and I held Titos in Grandma Lil's *special* interrogation room. My mind drifted to Titos and whatever became of him. I missed half of Kevin's lecture. I quickly snapped out of my thoughts and returned to the conversation.

"Please tell me where you are and what's going on? I only got bits and pieces from your grandma. She was very short on the phone."

"I'd rather not talk about things that make me want to throat punch someone."

Kevin was silent. I imagined him crossing his arms and glaring through me.

"Grandma Lil may have been breached and is speaking in code ... wait, *you* spoke to her? She was supposed to call me when she was clear."

"Your gran called me on accident. I guess she was testing her system. Anyway ... where are you?"

Out of the corner of my eye, I spotted something that made my shit show of a day, shittier.

"O'Malley. I gotta go," I said with gritted

teeth.

"You need to watch your six, Re—"

Click. I disconnected the call.

CHAPTER 21

Rage consumed me as heat rose to my face. Few things anger me in this world—yeah, okay, so most things pissed me off of late. But animal cruelty? That took the cake. I spotted a medium-sized female dog, similar to a Red Kelpie from the movie Red Dog. She dashed past me on the side street. She was yipping as she peered behind her. Her eyes were wild with fear and a rope bound tightly around her neck. She was surely escaping a certain hell.

As I edged out to follow her, a guy on a cheap old beach cruiser rode past, shouting, "Get back here, you stupid bitch. I'm gonna kill you!" He was your average tweaker with dirty, holey clothing, disheveled hair, pock marks on his face. He held what appeared to be a baton in his left hand. It was more like a night stick they issued cops back in the day.

I'd lost two friends that morning. I'd be damned if I let that dog be another statistic. I felt the veins in my neck protrude and my jaws tightened. I floored it and did a PIT maneuver. My department did not approve the Pursuit Intervention Technique, but I was dead, and homeless, and didn't give a flying rat's ass. It was something the infamous honey badger and I had in common.

I tapped the rear tire of the tweaker's bike, and he fishtailed, swerving left and right before straightening it out with the front tire wobbling. Impressive, I thought. He snapped a scowl over his shoulder, screamed profanities, and continued his pursuit of the poor pup. Okay, he did not take to my warning shot. So, I did what any sensible person would do ... I put pedal to the metal and struck him again. This time it worked. He hit the curb and went flying off his bike into the bushes. The night stick landed a few feet away. His rear tire was mangled.

Cars swerved and honked their horns at the commotion. I was in a zone. I slammed my brakes, yanked the wheel of my silver Jeep to the left and jumped the curb, stopping sharp. With the engine still running, I hopped out, leaving the door opened. My teeth were snarling when I bolted over and snatched the night stick from the ground. By this time, the shit bird hopped to his feet. He was flailing his arms, looking around for the dog. But she had taken off, hopefully to greener pastures.

As I approached him, his eyes were wide, and pupils the size of a pin. He was thrashing and pacing. I unleashed every profane word that came to mind and even made up a few. I'd forgotten about my recent injury in my rage and raised the stick above my head. With my crappy morning, I was itching to give him a beat down. But something held me back.

I stood, looking as crazy as he did. I flipped the hood of the sweatshirt over Copper's baseball cap and adjusted my Maui Jim aviators.

"So, you like to abuse animals!" I shouted and waved the stick at him. "You probably hit women and children too ... coward." I jumped at him. "You want a piece of someone? Come on, give me a shot!"

He flailed his arms, slapping his gums. "No, no, man, I don't have a beef with you. That fucking bitch dog bit me," he bellowed.

"Yeah, because you probably kick the shit out of her and leave her tied to a tree with no food or water," I thundered. It was something I'd seen too many times in my career. "You're probably pissed because you were gonna sell her as a bait dog ... you piece of shit." I slammed the stick on the ground next to him.

By now we had a crowd from the D's restaurant. I realized I was supposed to play it low key. This was opposite. And it'd be a matter of time before some loser posted it to YouTube or Facebook. I'd been there before, but I was drugged when I was filmed calling my former boss a "pencil dick twat waffle."

So, I lowered my head, flung the night stick at him, and hustled to the rental before someone identified me. Thank God it didn't have any plates. As I approached the Rubicon, I spotted a set of shaking furry ears over the dashboard.

He saw her too and shouted, "Hey, that's my dog."

I didn't turn around but yelled, "Not anymore. I'm taking the dog ... asshole." I gave him a stiff middle finger salute.

I slid behind the wheel and tore off, my head on a swivel for a tail. I wasn't paying attention, missed the Hwy 89 exit, and ended up on Interstate 80 toward Reno. "Crap," I shouted. I looked at the pup, who was riding shotgun, staring at me. "Sorry, girl. You've probably had enough ugly talk in your life." Instead of fear in her eyes, I could've sworn she flashed a smile.

As I eased my hand on the pooch, I felt around her neck and the rope was so tight it practically embedded in her skin. "Grr. I should've kicked the tweaker's ass." I furrowed my brows. I again was not paying attention as CA 267 approached quicker than I remembered. I took a hard right onto the exit. The dog flew across the seat onto the floorboard.

"Crap, crap, sorry girl," I said.

She wagged her tail. My erratic driving must not have fazed her.

After a few miles on 267, I crossed the Truckee River, passed the airport, and pulled to the side. "Humph. I've come full circle," I mumbled as I removed my knife from my fanny pack. After I gently severed the rope, I discovered scar tissue and exposed skin. I poured water on a napkin and softly dabbed her wounds. I looked in the front zippered section of my fanny pack and found a red paisley cowboy bandana and placed it around her neck.

She appeared to grin again and sat with her ears folded back. Her nose went into the air and she followed her scent to my burger. The bag had rolled under the seat during my mad rush to escape. She stuck her head in, ripped the paper and swallowed it whole. She most likely hadn't eaten in days.

"We'll figure this out, girl. I won't let anyone hurt you again," I cooed and slowly reached my hand over to pet her.

She stared at me with her big brown eyes and let out a loud burp. I couldn't help but laugh. After inhaling my food, she climbed back onto the seat and inched closer to me, placed her head on my shoulder, giving me smooches. It was something we both needed.

"I'm unsure what to do with you. I've been a lone wolf for a while. And I have no home. I'm on the run from some *very* bad people who, by the way, snatched my father." I drew a heavy sigh. "We will figure it out."

The little red dog cocked her head and pawed at the bag.

"Sorry, no more grub." I opened the bottle of water and gave her some. "Before we head to the secret squirrel zone, I need to get you food," I said. I put the car in drive and headed for a pet supply in Kings Beach.

"Better hold tight to your milk bones, it's about to get crazy," I said.

In reality, I had no idea what the rest of the day was going to bring me. My stomach churned.

CHAPTER 22

FBI Investigative Specialist Gretel Hendle stood outside Agent Powers's Palm Island home, disconnecting the call. She squinted as a federal agent pulled into the circular cobblestone driveway, driver's window down.

"Hey, brother." Gretel put on her happy face. "Didn't Agent Powers call you?"

"No," the Latino male agent replied, opening the car door.

"I'm sorry. They reassigned you to the Miami case." Gretel immediately slammed the door shut again and looked back at the house. She leaned in, rested her arms on the window edge. "The truth is, I promised Agent Powers I'd call you. He has so much on his plate," she said. "And, well, I dropped the ball. If he finds out, I'll never move up the ranks." She flashed the agent a toothy smile and flipped her long, wavy brown ponytail around.

Gretel stood, shoulders back, and opened the top two buttons of her FBI polo shirt, slowly and deliberately wiping the sweat from between her double Ds. "How do you deal with the Florida heat. It's kinda hot for May, don't ya think?" she said in a seductive tone.

He gawked at her breasts and swallowed hard. The agent shook his head and nodded at the house. "Are you sure? I ... I, um, had strict orders." The agent's Puerto Rican accent was strong.

"Come on, brother, don't get me in trouble here," she said, shoving her breasts in his face. "How about you and I grab a beer or two this weekend?" She licked her lips.

He cleared his throat. "O ... okay, but you promise you'll clear it with Powers. I don't need that dude pissed at me."

"Of course." Gretel ran her fingers over her heart, caressing her chest. "Cross my heart."

"It's a date." He raised his brows and pulled out of the driveway.

Gretel waved at the befuddled-looking agent, smiling widely. After he was out of sight, she rolled her eyes, shook her head in disgust, buttoning her shirt. "It's about fucking time," she mumbled.

She marched to the porch and pulled a Glock 9mm and a suppressor from her work bag. Since she was not in an armed position, she had to keep it hidden. Gretel attached the suppressor to the muzzle and strolled to the rear of the house. She approached the agent who stood guard on the east side. She looked around to make sure it was clear and shot him point blank in the back of the head. Gretel watched as he fell to his face on the neatly manicured lawn. She untucked her shirt and stuffed the gun in the waistband of her khaki 5.11s. She yanked the lifeless body by the ankles and dragged him deep into the bougainvillea shrub, hiding him as best she could.

She ducked under the backyard window and popped the second agent. "Two down, one more to go," she mumbled as she again jammed the pistol in her khakis, picked leaves off her shirt, and twirled her ponytail into a tight bun. As she made her way to the front of the house, she texted Chena. *On target.*

She put her best FBI game face on and strolled through the front door, where the final agent awaited his fate.

CHAPTER 23

We arrived at Kings Beach around 2:30 p.m. I bolted into the pet store and picked top-of-the-line kibble. I had to ease her into healthy food since no doubt shit-bird fed her crap, if anything at all. I was a kid in a candy store and grabbed doggie shampoo, a bed, snacks, a bone for her teeth, doggie antiseptic for her wound, and a squeaky soft monkey. As I stood in line, ready to use my credit card, it hit me. I'm dead and the deceased don't leave a digital trail. Playing dead and being on the run didn't come with an instruction manual. So, I pulled out the remaining cash and counted. Hmm. Sorry, red dog, just the essentials.

I hustled to my Jeep, pressed start, and idled in the parking lot. As I gazed out at the clear blue lake, watching tourists mill about, enjoying their unseasonably warm, sunny day, it occurred to me. Sue's parents lived ten minutes up the road in Incline Village. During college days, we'd take turns visiting one another's family for the holidays. I stroked her soft, cotton sweatshirt and tears welled in my eyes. I wiped them away.

Undoubtedly by now, Sue's parents heard the news of her murder, and friends and family were flocking to their house, offering condolences. I wanted with every inch of my crushed soul to be one of them. But what would I say? Sorry, it should've been me that was executed in the hotel room.

I let out a heavy sigh. "Not to mention, they probably heard about my house explosion and likely death. It would be too much for them." I plopped my head on the steering wheel and rolled my head to the dog. "It can't hurt to cruise by ... right?" I squinted at my furry friend for approval.

She wagged her tail and jammed her face in the plastic bag and pulled out a bone, her butt doing a jig. She closed her eyes and chomped away, not caring about anything else.

"Okay, but only a drive by," I mumbled and put the Jeep in drive, tearing down State Route 28. A few minutes later, I approached Lake Drive. My heart pounded, and my palms were sweaty. Was I really going to go there? What if they saw me? The shock would be too much.

I drove slow and steady as I turned right. "I can't do this. It's not right." I was about to make a U-turn until I peered to my right and spotted four men wearing dark suits and armed with AK-47s. One approached a black Escalade limo that had just pulled into a circular stone paved driveway.

Men holding heavy guns were not an everyday sight in Lake Tahoe. I let off the gas pedal and inched at a turtle's pace. One of the armed men opened the rear passenger door.

"No, it couldn't be. He looks like ... Max! What?" I said. My heart palpitated, and I swerved, running over the side curb.

The men glanced in my direction. "Crap, crap, crap." I yanked my hood over the hat and continued toward Sue's parents' house. No way ... maybe my eyes were playing tricks on me. I was tired. I shook my head and looked over at the dog, but she was too busy with her bone.

"Phew. Close call. Hopefully, they thought I was a lost tourist," I said.

I made a U-turn a couple of houses before Sue's folk's and pulled partially onto the sidewalk, parking on the opposite side of the street. But I couldn't see much. The men were standing behind a tall extravagant renaissance design wrought-iron gate. Privacy hedges and the stoned walls blocked my view, not to mention the massive pines that lined the driveway. It was a fortress.

The lakefront estate set back from the street and was an easy nine thousand square-feet. "Hmm, someone important must live there." I bit my lower lip as I contemplated. But my inquisitive nature took over common sense. "I got it. But you have to stay here, doggo," I said to her.

I flipped the hood off my head and adjusted my ponytail through the opening in the back of the hat. I assessed my wardrobe. It was a good thing I still wore my exercise clothes. But the blood-stained sweatshirt had a large hole in the left arm, I was still picking glass out of my hair, and my leggings were tattered. Okay, I looked more like a vagrant.

I flipped the visor down and studied myself in the mirror. Yikes! I dabbed Carmex on my lips with my ring finger and adjusted my Maui Jim glasses and pinched my cheeks. "I could pass for a runner, right?" I glanced at the dog.

I rolled down my windows for the dog and ordered her to stay. They were high enough so she shouldn't be able to jump out. My red hair was a dead giveaway, so I tucked my ponytail into the sweatshirt but kept the hat on and set out for a power walk. The instant I moved my left arm, it throbbed to a level eight, so I opted for a leisurely stroll. Fanny pack and all.

I remained on the opposite side of the street and the second I was in front of the estate, I caught a glimpse in between the gate, so I bent down feigning to tie my shoe. Out of the corner of my eye, I saw a woman with long, black hair with silver streaks, wearing a white pants suit. She was talking to the man I thought was Max. He had raven hair, wore dark glasses, and looked as if he stepped out of the tropics, with his elegant linen attire down to his undoubtedly over-priced loafers and a jacket he flung over one shoulder.

All parties were somber looking with forlorn faces. A third man stood next to Max. He was Hispanic and stood approximately five feet, ten inches. He had black hair, a black goatee and mustache, and appeared to be in his late fifties. He donned a fedora.

I scanned the driveway and spotted a vehicle with *Hospice* stenciled on the panel. I needed a picture and since my burner phone did not have a great camera, I took the chance with my personal iPhone. I zoomed in for a closer peek. Just then, the woman pulled out her cell from her pants pocket and strolled inside the house.

As I took multiple pictures, the armed men glanced my way. Sweat dripped down my tankini. The man who looked like Max also flipped his head in my direction. My blood pressure skyrocketed. It *was* Max! But how and why? He wore a sad expression and did not appear to be enjoying himself. The big clue was when one of the armed blokes shoved him at gun point. Max tripped going up the steps as he glanced at me.

Crap, he may have recognized me. I lowered my gaze and continued to speed walk, thrusting my arms, grimacing at the pain. Perhaps my judgment meter read *Stupid*, but it got worse and went clear to red. Moron level. What the heck? It wouldn't have been the dumbest thing I'd done all day. If I were a cat, I would've used up half my lives today. But I had a few remaining, so I meandered beyond the gated mansion, crossed the street and backtracked to the Rubicon on *their* side of the street.

I stopped on the west side of the mansion and peeked through the iron gates and spotted a private pier with a boat hoist leading to a swanky boat house. More armed men milled around the dock. My spine tingled. "Who are they guarding?" I whispered.

Suddenly, my heart fluttered, just like it did when I landed in Montana and my body prickled with goose bumps. I had to get closer. The gate was unlocked, so I did what any reasonably crazy person would do; I made my way through, keeping my head on a swivel.

I removed my cell again, taking multiple pictures. I snapped a shot of the house, the car, the back yard and stuffed it back in my running leggings. I also made a mental note of the lay out. There was another black sedan parked next to the hospice vehicle. This guy's as wealthy as Max.

As I slowly spun on my heels to return to the sidewalk, I bumped into the barrel of an AK-47.

CHAPTER 24

My body quivered as a ginormous man towered over me. He was an easy six feet, five inches. He had short, curly, blond hair, striking blue eyes, and bulging muscles, no neck. "What are you doing here? This is private property." His voice boomed as he shoved the rifle in my face.

Quick, act fast. "Uh ... I am so sorry." *What the hell? Where'd the country girl accent come from? Okay, just go with it.* "Ya see. I ... I" I tilted my head. I would have batted my eyelashes, but I was wearing sunglasses. "I can't find my aunt's dawg. She got out and ... I looked everywhere." I threw my arm out and touched my forehead. I guess now I'm a freakin' damsel in distress. "I'm sick to my stomach. If I lose her, my aunt will have my

hide. Ya see ... I'm visitin' her down the street."
I inclined my head toward Sue's parents.

"I don't care about your dog ... now move
along." He jutted his chin as he lowered the
barrel of the AK.

Phew! It worked. It appeared he didn't deem
me a threat. I pushed the envelope and tip
toed, peering around him into the courtyard.

"What's the dog's name?" he asked, stone-
faced, as he pressed his body against mine.

Oh, crap. Now he's testing me. I always push
the envelope until it busts through at the
seams. "Um ..." I bit my lower lip. I couldn't say
"Red Dog" ... think. I looked down the street at
Sue's parents and blurted the first name that
came to mind. "Sue." What was I thinking?
He'd never believe a dog named Sue. Hell, I
had a hard time believing myself.

"I didn't see a dog," he said with furrowed
brows. "What's your name?" He backed me
into the fence.

"Uh ... me?" I gestured to myself. "It's Amy."
Great, two dead friend's names. "I ... I promise.
I don't mean no harm." I yelled out for Sue,
praying my friend's family would not hear me. I
stepped away from the ogre. "Do you mind if I
look in your backyard?" I peeked around him,
the nape of my neck drenched.

"Yes, I mind, and you need to come with
me." He pulled my arm.

Just as he laid hands on me, the dog came
from behind him and growled, baring her
teeth. So she could jump out after all.

"Oh, my goodness. There you are ... you little

stinker." I pulled away and grabbed her by the bandana. I didn't know what she was capable of doing and did not want her getting the boot or worse yet, shot. I yanked on her and scampered off. "See ya. Thank you." I waved.

Poof, my accent was gone and so were we. I peeked down at the dog. "Hmm. Is your name really, 'Sue'?" She looked up at me and wagged her tail, probably thinking this was a fun game.

I trembled the entire trek back to the Jeep. I jumped in, pressed *Start*, and sped away. Again, I peered in the rearview and side mirrors, looking for a tail. And not the furry kind the dog was wagging. My right hand bore nail impressions from the vice grip on the steering wheel. A sudden rush and searing pain pierced my heart. Who was he? And what the hell was going on?

When we were a safe distance, I dialed O'Malley on my burner phone, but it went straight to voicemail. I left a message. I called Grandma, but the same recording played. In cases like this, James was my go-to guy. I scrolled through my newly programmed contacts and found AP, my silly Austin Powers nickname for him. I paused before I hit *Call*. My inner voice objected. AP had enough on his plate with a new job and a baby on the way. I clicked the right-side button of the cell, and the screen went black. I continued on to Homewood.

CHAPTER 25

Max snarled at the goon with the AK-47 as he shoved him into the threshold of SJ's mother's house. The hair on the scruff of his neck stood erect as Max knew the chances of him leaving feet first were high. He peered out the window as the giant talked to the woman. There was something familiar about her voice that made his spine tingle. Could it be *her*? He wasn't certain. She wore sunglasses. But one thing, her red hair was recognizable, even sticking out of that hat.

The ogre entered.

"Who was she?" Max asked.

"Someone looking for her dog. Now move," the goon said as he pushed Max into the living room.

Max spun and threw his jacket on the floor.

"Touch me again and see what happens," he said in a low growl.

The man glared.

"That's enough, Archer!" SJ shouted.

Max tugged at the tails of his shirt, snatched his Gucci, and stepped away from the confrontation. He considered Archer's height and weight. It would not be a fair fight. He turned and noticed Chena on the back deck, pacing as she spoke on the phone. Her brows wrinkled. It was obvious things were not going her way.

Just then, a priest came down the stairs and whispered something in SJ's ear.

SJ's eyes widened. "Watch him, Archer," he said, bolting up the stairs.

Archer grunted.

Few things would get SJ to move that fast. It must be his mother. On the plane ride to Tahoe, SJ divulged to Max his mother was dying, and her last wish was to see him. The priest must've read her last rites. Did SJ make it in time?

Max stood in the living room, the floors echoed beneath his feet. If he were a voluntary visitor, he would've appreciated the marble floors with the vaulted ceilings, the carved mahogany handrails, cherry wood credenza with matching bar. Even the furnishings were classic. Only things missing were framed pictures and any other personal items. Max surmised since her ex-husband and son were part of the cartel, fuzzy family photos were not on display for the world to see.

But Max was very unwelcomed and kept an eye out for an escape. He could just tiptoe out the door. No, that wouldn't work. SJ had armed men everywhere. Max cursed himself for getting on the helicopter, but his own private henchman, D.O.G. was in Mazatlán with Lucy for the day. D.O.G. most likely had no clue Max went missing. He needed to get a message to him, but they took his laptop the minute he exited the plane in Tahoe.

As he contemplated, a chill cut through him, so he shrugged into his coat. His linen apparel was no match for the Lake Tahoe elements. Just then Chena entered. Max overheard "Miami" and "Gretel" before she hung up. Perhaps he could talk the information out of her. What was the plan for him? Were they going to torture him the way they were Teddy?

Chena stared. "Well, Max. We meet again."

"I wish it was under better circumstances. I'm just going to ask you outright. What the hell am I doing here?" He stood with hands on his hips, his leg back.

"That's up to SJ. It's out of my control. He's the shot caller." She moved to the bar and poured herself a drink.

He looked at his watch. Three o'clock.

"It's close enough to five ... would you like?"

"Why not? I'll have a martini, shaken, two olives. A little dirty," he said matter-of-factly.

Chena shot a scowl. "I'm not a freaking bartender. Here's a scotch." She leaned forward and sniffed. "New cologne?"

"I was tired of the old one and had another

formulated for me. Less musky. Not that it matters now." He snarled and snatched the drink. After he gulped it down, he bared his teeth and shook his head. Max presented his tumbler for a second malty pour.

"Bad day?" Max asked. "I know mine is a *nightmare.*" He glared at her.

Chena poured Max another. "I just got word it's about to get better." She raised her glass.

"What's the good news?" Max fished and threw back the second. He handed it over for a third pour of liquid courage.

She obliged Max's request. "Well, it won't do any harm to tell you. I have a person on the inside in Florida. Rose's sisters are under a very watchful eye. If the Ghost fails to produce, they will be eliminated."

"What do you mean, *sisters*? I thought you were dealing with Teddy. Are you saying Rose is alive?" Max's heart palpitated.

She drew a deep breath, sauntered away, and remained silent.

Max's assumption was correct. His beloved was still among the living. And this Gretel person from Miami was watching her sisters. He patted his pockets and felt for his phone. He had to get the word out to someone, anyone. Then it hit him.

"Where's the bathroom?" he asked Chena.

CHAPTER 26

"Cell phone," Chena said, snapping her fingers and holding out her hand.

"Seriously?" Max looked at her snapping fingers and back to her gaze. "Who the hell am I going to call? The police? And say, 'Hey, my name is Max and I'm a fugitive from justice who's being held against his will. Come arrest me.' And besides, your goons took it from me ... along with my freaking laptop," Max said with a shrug and stomped away. He discovered the bathroom on his own. He entered, closed the door and quickly locked it.

Max leaned on the sink with his hands firmly placed on the granite countertop and shook his head at himself in the oval wood mirror. "What happened to you? No one pushes you around," he said. Rage washed over him. Max paced the bathroom and weighed his options. They did not look good. Prison, a slow painful, agonizing death like they were doing to Teddy, or a quick shot to the head. Whatever he chose, he was not going down without a fight.

Boom, *boom*. A pounding on the door interrupted his pep talk. "Hey, what the hell are you doing in there?" Archer yelled from the other side.

"None of your damn business. Now leave me the fuck alone," Max shouted for the first time. He pulled the cell from his pants' pocket and dialed the one person in the world he swore as his enemy. "Perhaps I can make a deal?" he mumbled.

"Shit, voice mail." He held his hand over the mouthpiece and stepped to the opposite end of the powder room. "It's Max," he said in a hushed voice. "I know I'm the last person you'd expect to hear from. I have to make this short. I'm at SJ's mother's home in Incline Village. He's one of your targets. I'm pretty sure Teddy is here somewhere, too. There is a mole in Florida. A woman named Gretel. This is not a joke. Maybe we can cut a deal, but you have to hurry. Trace the phone if you want. I give you full permission."

Another loud bang. "Open the damn door, or I'm breaking it down," Archer shouted.

Max flushed the toilet. "Excuse me ... can't a person have any privacy?" he said. He shot his eyes around the bathroom, looking for a place to hide the phone. He could stick it in between the cushions of the fainting couch. No, that wouldn't work. And then he saw it sitting on the windowsill, a dusty vase. Max wrapped the cell in toilet paper and gently lowered it to the bottom and rushed back to the sink.

The handle jostled, followed by keys, and the door flung wide, slamming against the wall.

The blood rushed to Max's face. He squared off with Archer, clenched fists. One thing his evil stepfather taught him was how to take a beating.

CHAPTER 27

Forty-five minutes later, we arrived in the West Shore. It was a quarter to four when I veered off CA 89, turning right onto a fire road, just between Homewood and Tahoma. The road was unsuspecting, and no one would think twice about cruising it. Approximately two and a half uphill miles on hard packed dirt road, mixed with snow, we arrived at the family safe house.

Grandma Lil's cabin was deep in the moss-covered dense green forest and obscured by rows of various pines and white firs. The five acres was backed by hundreds of forested acres and set southwest of the ski resort. Since the cabin did not officially exist, there wasn't a street address. Hell, Google Earth couldn't locate it. All part of Grandma's plan.

Grandma's cabin was 1,250 square-feet, but the actual living quarters was closer to seven hundred and fifty. The cabin was tucked away from public. If one were to stumble across it, it was best to turn back. There were signs declaring *Private Property, No Trespassing, Violators will be Prosecuted* posted. It was off the grid. There were no power lines going into the house. Grandma used a state-of-the-art quiet generator.

The cabin was barren in front. Grandma did not have any plants, attractive rocking chairs or a *Welcome to our Cabin* mat. That was the point. No one was welcomed unless invited. And she certainly did not keep up on the stain. The cabin was raw and downright frightful. It bore the likeness of a haunted house in a horror movie.

The two front and north-facing windows were barred. They also had bullet-proof panels on the inside that sealed with a press of a button in an emergency. The south and rear facing windows were permanently sealed. The cabin's only exposed entrance was the front door. But it was a façade. The red door was fortified and did not open.

To the naked eye, the cabin was inaccessible. The only entrance was through a concealed garage on the north side. Sue Dog and I made our way around to the side where car tracks stopped. Or so it appeared, thanks to Grandma's designers, who, like most of her staff, signed non-disclosure contracts. I parked, jumped out of the Jeep, and found a hidden panel on the north side and slid it open. I punched in a code and one final password, *Violet Lee*. It was a combination of my mother's name and maternal grandmother's middle name.

The faux siding opened like a garage door. I crept in and parked next to the only other vehicle, a camouflaged four-seater, side by side and killed the engine. The garage was long and narrow.

Sue Dog and I jumped out. She took a quick tinkle and looked at me with a tilted head and caught a case of the zoomies. Her butt dropped, ears back, and she was off and wildly running. Another smile fell across her face. After her romp in what remained of the snow, I quickly shut the garage door.

Once I entered the code, the interior door leading into the cabin immediately unlocked for quick access. A small mudroom was the first room off the garage. It led directly into the kitchen. I flipped on the switch for the generator and stepped inside.

I stopped dead in my tracks. Someone was here.

CHAPTER 28

Dishes sat on the bamboo drying rack, but not a drop of water remained. I was certain I put everything away the last time I was here, a few months ago. My heart raced. I dropped the dog's bag of goodies and drew my gun from my fanny pack holster. I phoned Grandma but heard the same damn recording. Lily was next.

"Crap, straight to voicemail," I said to Sue Dog. Her hackles were not raised, nor did she appear to sense any threat. But she was on my heels.

The only people who knew about the cabin were Grandma, Lily, and myself, or so I'd thought. The cabin was cold, so whoever was here had no plans to return anytime soon. Out of habit, I had to clear the place.

I started downstairs with my weapon out, feet shoulder width apart, knees slightly bent, and torso forward, ready to engage my adversary. The wood floor creaked beneath my footsteps. Despite the outside appearance, the cabin was charming on the inside with the wide-plank knotty pine interior. The kitchen had a breakfast nook, a small table with two chairs. The main room had a brown leather sofa with matching recliner and a small coffee table in front.

An antique wood desk sat against the wall and neatly tucked in the corner was a twenty-two-inch LED monitor for the closed-circuit television surveillance cameras that were strategically placed around the cabin. The CCTV was Grandma's doing.

On the opposite side was an electric fireplace set in front of the real one. No fires allowed. It defeated the purpose of hiding.

I cleared it in one fell swoop, checking behind the couch and the only bathroom located downstairs. Next was upstairs. It was an open loft with one king bed, nightstand and a six-drawer chest of drawers. All honey pine, solid wood.

Since there were no threats, I re-holstered my weapon. Sue Dog had followed me the whole time and sniffed under the bed for any bad guys. We returned downstairs and went to the fully stocked kitchen. I poured the thirsty pup some water in a bowl and set it down.

I flipped on the electric heater that was next to the refrigerator. Although it was early May, it was cold. The cabin was deep in the woods, with no sun reaching it.

Last, but not least, was gather supplies. I opened the double door walk-in pantry that backed up to the garage. The light automatically went on overhead, and I promptly checked for intruders. I kicked myself as it should've been part of my sweep. Note to self, train more. Nonetheless, I breathed a sigh of relief, no one was there.

The pantry had four shelves on three sides filled with dried and canned goods, packets of Meals Ready to Eat, and ample water. The middle shelf had more than just the packets of MREs. I slid the shelf to the left. It revealed a control panel to another room. I flipped open the metal compartment and placed my face to the machine. Lights flickered and scanned my eyes. It was a Biometric Iris Scanner, just like the one at my grandmother's main house.

The fortified door opened. I stepped inside. The fireproof cave ran the length of the garage and took up a good chunk of the square footage. I know a bit overkill, but with Grandma, nothing was never enough.

The cave had everything one needed in case of an emergency. If today didn't count as an emergency, I couldn't imagine what would. A nuclear holocaust? The cave was essentially a bug out room. It contained extra clothing, snowshoes, boots, medical first aid kit, and a plethora of medications for any ailment.

On the other side was the fun gear: extra ammo, ballistic vests, helmets with night vision goggles, and assorted handguns and AR-15s. The contents would make any prepper look twice.

In the far back was a shelf with extra cash, prepaid Visa cards, and a Canadian passport with my picture and a bogus name. Again, I never questioned Grandma. I grabbed some cash and put it in my pack. An encrypted laptop sat on the shelf under it. Next to it was a soft computer case with a file containing Grandma's secret squirrel contacts and passwords for various websites for tracking people.

As I pulled it down, three pictures fell. I picked them up and my heart swelled. They were of Bradley and me standing in front of our home. I thumbed through them and smiled. Our realtor had taken them the day we closed escrow. Both—husband and home—now gone for good.

I slid to the floor and plopped my head in my hands, overwhelmed by despair. But I sucked back a stifled sob and wiped my tears with my sleeve. I couldn't let my sorrow cloud my mission.

I pondered. This was the only safe place I had left. I didn't know how much of my home had been destroyed by the bomb and fire.

I wanted my ring to be safe if something happened. It was the only thing left of Bradley, so I removed my wedding band and set it on the pictures. In an odd way, I felt as if I were letting go of my husband. I sighed.

And then it hit me. My father did the same

thing with his watch and the photos at the crash site. I took them out of my pack and stared at them and reflected on the video. Nothing made sense. I removed the watch and examined it. Just broken and non-assuming, or so I'd thought. So, I stuck it back on and left all the pictures together in the safe room.

Just then Sue Dog scampered in, sniffed me and sneezed. She put her paw on my foot and looked at the kitchen.

"I get the hint. I'll feed you and take a shower."

CHAPTER 29

"Hey, babe," James said. "Good news. They re-scheduled training. I'm headed back to the house. I still can't get a hold of your grandma or Rose. I'm not happy with this little family *protocol*. They should've let my department deal with it." He sighed.

"I'm sick to my stomach too. I feel ... well, kind of like a mushroom," Saki said.

"Huh?" James tilted his head at the speaker.

"You know, kept in the dark and fed shi ... oops, crap. It would make me feel better if I knew what was happening."

"Yeah ... me too. I'll try to get a hold of Kevin again to se—" Just then James's phone beeped with an incoming call. He looked at the caller ID. It was blocked. He shrugged it off.

"I hear your phone. You need to get it?" Saki asked.

"Nah, I'll check the voicemail," he said. "You're more important." James smiled widely.

"So, Gretel has been absolutely amazing. She even let a couple of the agents go early," Saki said.

"She did what!? That is *not* her call. She is not an agent and has no authority." James growled.

"I'm sure there are more on the outside perimeter. And Kaylee is here. I'm fine. I'll see you when you get home. I love you," Saki said.

"I'll be there in an hour, tops. I love you more," James said as he disconnected. He dialed another number. The FBI agent who was scheduled to be at the house.

"It's Powers, where are you?" he asked gruffly.

"Uh, Hendle said you called me off ... didn't you?" the agent said nervously with the Latin accent.

"Negative! Now get your ass back to my house, stat," James barked and disconnected.

He hit his voicemail message. What the hell? Max? James listened with furrowed brows. He clenched his jaws and stomach tightened. James flipped on his emergency lights and sirens and slammed his foot on the accelerator. He called his wife again.

CHAPTER 30

After a quick snack of nuked chicken-noodle soup and a much-needed shower, I dressed in jeans, a black turtleneck, black oversized sweatshirt, and black tactical boots. I wrapped a bag around my arm to avoid the stitches getting wet and scrubbed my hair. I hurriedly blew my hair dry and tied it into another ponytail. The best part of having a "bug out cabin" is that it had *all* the essentials, including toiletries. Sue Dog even got a cleaning. I was surprised when she jumped in the shower on her own. Her zoomies afterward gave me a chuckle.

I plopped at the desk, opened the encrypted laptop, and conducted a records search of the Incline Village mansion. The listed owner was Annaliese Albrecht, mid-nineties, on hospice.

The home was in the Albrecht family trust. The information on the limo was blocked. So, I used Grandma's secret squirrel search engine and completed the backdoor quest. The vehicle was registered to an LLC out of Reno, AA Corp. "Most likely a shell company." I mumbled. But the AA Corp. looked familiar to me.

I dialed Grandma again. She was still on lockdown. I'd hoped it would end soon. Morbid curiosity took over, so I checked personal and work emails and even went to the chatter room. The rumors flew I was rogue, AWOL, and a person of interest in the murder of my friend. But most believed I blew up with my house. Ugh. I shut my laptop screen and leaned back, rubbing my arm. Just then, the wicker basket fell over.

After Sue Dog's bathing, she was in a playful, mischievous mood and was rooting in the trash. "What are you doing?" I asked in a high-pitched, playful voice. She looked at me with wide eyes, yipped, and scampered off shaking in the corner. This poor pup had been so abused she probably got beat for everything she did or didn't do wrong.

I slid down next to the couch and patted on the oriental red carpet that laid under it and covered part of the living room. "Come on, baby girl. I will never hurt you," I cooed in baby talk.

Sue Dog cowered and approached me in a belly crawl. She rolled over submissively with her tail tucked under her butt.

"Who's a good girl?" I squealed again.

She rolled back over and inched closer, giving me kisses. I got the feeling she was beginning to believe I'd never hurt her. "You are more trusting than me, dog."

As I began to put the crumpled paper in the basket, it occurred to me. This was *not* my trash. I stopped and dumped it all back on the carpet. There were at least six balls of paper. I smoothed out the crinkles and flattened them out. I stared with an open mouth, my hands trembled, and my heart pounded.

"Oh. My. God!" Tears poured down my face. I gazed at six letters, unfinished:

My Dearest Rosebud:

I don't know where to begin. The last time you saw me, you were seven. I question if I did the right thing, putting family second over the interest of others. If I could do it over again, I would not. Please forgive me. I am doing one final job. I want to be a better grandfather than I was a father ...

I was on my knees like a kid opening Christmas presents, waiting for the ultimate gift as I read each one. They were more of the same. Apology letters. "These are dated a week ago. He was here, but how and why?" I slumped with my head on my knees.

Sue Dog laid down and faced me like a jack rabbit. Her ears perked and eyes trained on me, hanging on my every word.

As I pet her, it occurred to me. If this sweet, ill-treated dog could learn to trust and forgive after all the abuse, I could too. I needed to forgive my father and let go of the resentment, like Grandma said. I'd absolved him in my mind, but my heart held on to an ugly bitterness. I was done living in the past. I had to start living in the present, like Sue Dog.

My phone buzzed. It was Copper giving me the address of the meeting place. I stood. "Let's roll, doggo."

CHAPTER 31

Ⅰt was five o'clock when I pulled up to the bar and grill. "Stay here this time," I said to Sue Dog, leaving the windows even higher. I exited my rented Jeep and stood in front of Toby's Hideaway, named after the owner, Tobias Tran. Copper gave me the 411. Toby's was a stone's throw from Lake Street and so well-hidden off the main highway, you'd pass it and not give it another look. Toby's catered more to locals than tourists, not that vacationers were unwelcomed, just not invited. Copper told me there was a reserved room in the back for "special guests."

I pushed through the heavy wood door into the dimly lit atmosphere. Toby Keith played at a moderate level in the background. As soon as my eyes adjusted to the low light, I gazed around the tavern and noted the décor was eclectic and outdated, but clean, with no stale beer smell. Five small round tables were at the front and four high tops lined the east side of the wall. The bathrooms were at the far back.

On the opposite side, a curved mahogany bar ran the length of the room. Mirrors backed it. The bar rail had elephant head rail holders. Behind the cash register was a wall dedicated to military and law enforcement patches. All tastefully done. Nine barstools sat in a neat L shape, only one occupied at the far end closest to the register. Swinging double doors led to what I assumed was the grill part of the bar.

The moment I entered, the sole patron turned his head and quickly scanned me. It was either my imagination or he wore a grimace. But after my day, any peculiar look in my direction gave me pause. The man wore a black baseball cap, jeans, and boots, with a black worn leather jacket. He returned to his tumbler. The man's eyes followed me in the mirror behind the bar.

I bit my lip and tried not to stare back.

Another man stood behind the bar, cleaning glasses. He wore blue jeans, and a black fitted t-shirt with the bar's name printed on the front. He was fit without being overly muscular and stood my height. He had gentle, light brown, almond-shaped eyes, was most likely in his early fifties, with black, crew cut hair. He was of Vietnamese heritage.

"You must be Rose," he said.

"Yes, I am." I raised a brow. "How'd you

know?"

"You've got the po-po scan." He chuckled. "I've seen your same assessing sweep on L.E.s that come in. And I was given your description," he said, walking out from behind the bar.

"You must be Tobias Tran."

He smiled, extending his hand. "Call me Toby." Toby had a gentle, calm nature about him. But judging by the scars on his face and arms, he'd probably seen his share of action. From the looks of the American flag and Semper Fi that hung high above the bar, I'd guess Toby also served. He most likely doubled as his own bouncer, and undoubtedly had a weapon tucked behind the bar in the event things got wild.

"Um, random question. Do you allow dogs?" I asked.

He tilted his head. "Huh?"

"I promise, she's well behaved and is waiting in my vehicle." I pointed to the door.

"Are you sure?" He glanced behind me then returned to the bar, resuming his duties.

I turned. Sue Dog was doing the happy dance, wagging her tail.

"How—"

"We have a back door. The meeting room is also there. And ... yes, we allow some dogs, as long as they don't bite. I'm referring to the two-legged type." Toby smiled as he examined a freshly washed beer mug. "But if the health inspector comes in, it's a service dog, right?"

"Oh ... absolutely," I said and took the last

stool at the end of the bar, opposite the other guy. I studied his features. I placed him in his early forties. He wore an old man's scowl, yet too young to be called "crotchety." I'd say more of a curmudgeon.

Just as Toby handed me a menu, a young gal with shoulder length, wavy auburn hair and brown eyes emerged through the double swinging doors, carrying a plate of wings. I estimated her to be Kaylee's age. She stood an inch taller than me and had an athletic, lean body with a dimply smile. She placed the plate in front of the curmudgeon.

"Thanks, Elly May," he uttered his first words without cracking a smile.

Elly May suited her. She smiled and approached me. "What'll ya have?" she asked with a southern drawl.

While I contemplated, Sue Dog jumped on the bar stool next to me.

Toby, Elly May, and I shook our heads and laughed.

"I'm sorry, I'll take her down," I said.

"Let her stay. She's a doll," Elly May said, bopping the dog's nose.

"My friend will have a bowl of water if that's okay."

"You got it," Toby said and returned to the kitchen.

While I perused the menu, Elly May gave me a rundown on her life. She moved from the Ozarks with her boyfriend and was navigating through life. She was twenty-two and attending Sierra Nevada College in Incline. While she enjoyed all the outdoor activities Lake Tahoe offered, she missed the hunting back home.

I gave her a nod. "I get it."

Just then, the bar's door opened, and the dog let out a low growl with her hackles raised.

"I'll have a Tito's, tonic," I said, leaning into Sue Dog to quell her.

"Aww, you miss me that much, doll?" A familiar voice echoed.

I spun my stool. My mouth dropped. I immediately jumped to my feet. Since I'd ditched my fanny pack holster, I reached under my sweatshirt for my concealed pistol.

CHAPTER 32

Max spread prone on the ground with one punch. He bolted to his feet. "Is that all you got?" He rubbed his jaw where the ogre socked him. Max was grateful for that last shot of alcohol.

Archer looked at Chena and threw his arms out to her and curled his lip.

"Really, now you want to act like a drunk frat boy, Max?" Chena leaned against the wall and shook her head.

It was not Max's intention to be pummeled, but he needed a distraction away from the hidden cell phone.

Archer yanked Max by his jacket collar and reared his hand for another wallop.

Chena held her hand to him. "He is SJ's guest. Let him decide."

"Leave him be for now," SJ said from the top of the stairs. He made his way down, his head held low.

Max wrenched away from Archer's death grip.

"I leave in an hour," SJ said to Chena.

"I can be packed and ready to g—"

"No. This is your mess, you finish it," SJ said. "I came here to say goodbye." He looked up the stairs. "And I did."

"My condolences, sir," Chena said with a slow nod.

"Not necessary. All part of life," he said with his gaze fixed on Max.

"I'm also sorry for your loss, Stanley, er ... uh, SJ ... but I still don't understand why you brought me here. And I don't buy the whole 'insurance' story. Look, I held up my end of our deal. You have the Ghost. And from what I gather, he gave you the information." Max crossed his arms and glared.

"Maxwell, you don't understand. Your blunder delayed me six months and cost me *millions*. All over this ... redhead." SJ's accent was thick.

Max turned away.

SJ slammed his hand on the railing. "Look at me when I speak!" he shouted.

Max slowly returned his attention to SJ and was inches from his face. "Do you think you are the only one who lost money?" he asked slowly and deliberately. "I've sat on my hands for *six* months without conducting any business. I was perfectly fine until you people entered my life."

He held SJ's gaze.

The second Max inched closer to SJ, Archer and another equally large, bald man pushed in front of him. Each with an AK slung down the front of their bodies. They stood on opposite sides of Max like giant bookends, gripping his arms.

"Maxwell ... did you really need to ask me why I brought you here?" SJ said, squeezing Max's face and patting his cheeks. "You are inconsequential to me." SJ flicked his wrist in a dismissal way.

The men yanked Max off his feet and dragged him out the back door.

CHAPTER 33

"What the hell are you doing here, Titos?" I stood with my hand gripped tight to my weapon on my hip holster, waiting to see if he would reach for his.

"Whoa, take it easy, doll-face." Titos flashed a smug grin as his six foot four, over two-hundred-pound body took up the entire doorframe. He held his right hand to me in surrender, and gave a wave to Toby with his prosthetic left. "Hey, Toby. How you doin'?" His hazel eyes crinkled in the corners. Titos sounded like a mobster from the Bronx, rather than a former FBI agent.

Toby placed the water bowl down for Sue Dog. "Tony Titianos. Good to see you, my old friend," he said, stepping from behind the bar.

He ambled over and gave Titos a bro hug and handshake. He turned to me. "I see you two know one another. That must be an interesting story."

Titos and I glared at each other. "Humpf. You have noooo idea." I studied his every move and scanned him from head to toe. He looked healthier since our last encounter, bulkier, like our first meet and greet in Miami.

Sue Dog popped off her bar stool and walked around Titos, hackles up, but her teeth remained hidden. She sniffed around his left prosthetic leg.

Seriously, dog? Not even a growl. I considered and relaxed my shoulders. "Wh … what are you doing here?"

"Copper didn't tell ya? Crazy dame." He smoothed his buzzed cut brown hair.

"*What*?! So, *you* are Grandma's 'friend'?" I said with air quotes.

He smiled widely with his arms out. "I'm the dude," he said, gesturing to himself.

"*You* are the one leading the team?" I squinted.

"Not *leading*, just playin' puppet master." Titos shot a look to the bar. "Ya mind if I join ya?" He moseyed over and hopped on the stool. "Corona, please," he said.

Sue Dog jumped up next to him.

"Traitor, dog," I mumbled under my breath as I made my way back to my bar stool. "New leg?" I asked Titos.

"Yep … better prosthetics. I'm officially the bionic man. Ya wanna see?"

"Pass," I said.

The thought of looking at his artificial limbs brought back a gruesome reminder of that ill-fated day in the Keys where he took my partner, James, to feed him to two hungry crocodiles. But Titos got the raw end of the deal when a croc snapped, dragged, and rolled him, biting off part of his arm and leg. The crunching sounds still seared in my brain. I shook my head.

Toby handed Titos a beer.

"I ran into some money ... but I don't have to tell ya." He winked.

I stared at his choice of alcohol. "No hard stuff?"

"Nah, I don't drink as heavy as I used to. Life is freakin' great for me now."

I took a sip and turned to him. "Aren't you dead and were supposed to have disappeared?"

"Yeah, until your granny called me. We had this arraignment when she cut me loose. She could call on me, no questions asked. I owe her ... so here I am to help," he said. "All two hundred and thirty pounds of sexiness. My new bionic limbs weigh a little less."

"You may owe her, but not me," I retorted.

Elly May was cleaning the counter and stopped. She leaned over, resting her elbows on the bar, her chin on her hands. "I see there's history between you two, sounds like a fun story," she said.

"It's a long story, and it appears as if history is repeating itself," I said, rolling my eyes so far back I almost fell off my stool.

Titos and I both nodded and sipped our drinks at the same time.

"But I tell ya. This dame has a great right hook and can shoot like Annie fuckin' Oakley."

"And he was a rogue FBI agent," I said, looking at Elly May.

"Really?" He turned to face me. "Who kidnapped me in Montana? And fed me illegal shit?"

"You're so toxic you need a warning label!" I scowled. "And ... *if* you recall, you had my husband murdered, and you stalked me." I looked at my Tito's and tonic. "You even spiked my drink. I thought I was going insane ... and now you're on my *fucking* side?" I said drawing a deep breath. "*You* also shot and killed Jessie ... missing me by inches. It's a good thing you're dead ... because you're sure not pretty enough for prison." My voice was hard.

"*Wow*! Feel better?" he asked.

"No! I promised Saki I'd stop swearing ... and I don't like ugly talk. But you bring it out in me."

"I like it better when you swear." Titos slid me some peanuts. "Nuts?"

"Just a bit unhinged." I gave him a shit-eating, closed-mouth grin.

"You're pretty hot when you're pissed ... anyway, water under the bridge .... *Agent* O'Brien," he said and raised his beer to me. "For the record, I did not murder your husband. The truth is, Jessie was supposed to *disable* his vehicle to scare him. Not kill him ... stupid kid." He lowered his head. "I am truly sorry."

"So why did you pop Jessie?" I asked.

He took a swig. "Loose ends," he said coldly, with a far-off stare.

Sue Dog sat on the stool between us, ping ponging her head as if she understood our conversation.

I sipped my drink again and forced back the sob I felt emerging. "Well, I'm no longer an agent, at least for now. And ..."

The door opened again.

"I'm dead ... like you," I said, turning my head.

"Yeah, your da hottest dead chick I ever did see." Vino stood in the doorway with a Cheshire cat grin. "Hey, Cuz ... how they hanging?" He moseyed to the bar.

"Hey ... Vino Mohr, leaving the ladies wanting more," Titos chanted with a laugh. "Ya know they're hanging, down and a bit to the left." Titos stood and grabbed his junk.

Vino and Titos did a complicated greeting involving fists, hands, and shoulder bumps. Vino stood six inches shorter than his cousin.

Titos stepped back. "But I tell ya ..." He pointed to me. "This one here almost made one disappear into neva neva land. Ha," he said. "You remember, Sweet Cheeks, when you kicked me in da boys?" He adjusted his pants. "I still hurt thinking about it."

I shifted my gaze from Vino to Titos. "Holy crap! So, this is hell? Now I know why you looked familiar, Vino. You guys really cousins?"

"Yep, we are," they said in unison.

"So, how's da family?" Titos asked.

"*You?* Have a family?" I asked.

"Yep, a boy and girl, twins," he said as he stood on his toes and grabbed his belt. "I got me a nice Italian Catholic. Wit a big ra—" Vino grabbed his breasts.

"I get the picture." I raised my hand and closed my eyes. Trying to erase the image from my frontal lobe. I imagined I was in the movie *My Cousin Vinny*, but instead it was *Vino*.

Vino turned to me. "Hey, I am a faithful guy and can read from da menu. Anyway … how's the rest of your day been shaken' tootsie?" he asked.

"Peachy freakin' keen," I said.

Titos snorted. "Riight, by what her granny told me, it's been a shit-clown-show of epic proportion. I think her guardian angel asked for a job change. Trouble follows this gal." He threw a thumb at me. "She can't even go to a conference with a bunch of cops without shit happening to her." He chugged his beer.

"Can you *try* to have some compassion … for a second?" I asked with a scrunched face.

"Women, you can't live without 'em …" Vino said.

"And their bones ain't no good for soup," Titos finished the sentence.

"Was your gene pool chlorinated?" I flipped them off and slammed the rest of my drink. I turned to Elly May, and another was waiting.

"Shall I keep 'em coming?" she asked.

"No, thanks. Two is my limit. We've got work to do."

Just then the door opened, and we all flipped our heads.

Copper strode through like a Valkyrie ready for battle.

CHAPTER 34

"You're a sight for sore eyes." I slid off the stool and met her at the door. "Thank God someone else who doesn't have to grab their wankers every time they talk," I said with a raised voice, smirking at the bar.

Sue Dog followed and sniffed Copper, wagging her tail.

Copper pointed down. "A friend of yours?" she asked.

"Yeah, for now ... long story, but I'll need to find her a home once this is all done."

She plopped against me and stared up with sad eyes, whimpering.

"Let me know how it works for you. It appears she chose you," Copper said.

I looked at Sue Dog's sweet, fury face,

143

considered and shook it off. "I've had quite the afternoon."

"No doubt. Let's chat. The rest of the team will meet in the back. They're on a ride and should arrive any minute. We have a new intel guy on the team—well, not new. He's just returned. He's the best. As soon as we're caught up, you can come—"

"Don't leave me out of this, it's *my* father we're looking for," I said.

"I promise. We won't. We need to finish prior business. Then I'll come get you."

Resignation warred with my need to be in control. I finally surrendered. "Okay." I ran my hand along the stitches.

"How's the arm?" she asked.

"I'm fine, it's time for meds ... speaking of, how is Mia?"

"Down for the rest of this mission," Copper said. "She's resting in the South Shore. Butterfly has a cabin there and is tending to Mia as we speak. Mild concussion. It's a good thing Mia has a hard noodle."

Just then, rumbling vibrated the wood floor beneath our feet. I looked to see if the lights were swaying.

"Ha, no earthquake. The guys are here. They've got old school kick-start choppers. They were blowing off some steam," she said and took off for the back room.

I watched as Titos, Vino, and the curmudgeon followed Copper.

Sue Dog and I returned to the bar. My hunger button went off and stomach growled so loud it sounded like another approaching chopper. I asked for a double order of wings for myself and two plain hamburger patties for the dog. I was taking playing it dead to another level. There went my waistband.

A few minutes later, Elly May served our food. I salivated as I dove in mouth first, not coming up for air. Sue Dog did too. She wolfed her burgers, looked over and burped, staring at my plate. She was growing on me.

"Don't get used to this kind of food. *If* I'm going to keep you, there won't be much tavern food in your future. It'll be homemade," I said, scratching behind her ears.

By this time Toby's had more patrons milling about, so I paid no attention to anyone entering, pretty sure I blended in with the others. I drummed my fingers on the bar, waiting for Copper to call me in. Just as I finished my last tasty, spicy wing, my phone vibrated with an incoming text from an unknown number. I wiped my hands and swiped the screen. *Your boot's untied.*

"What the hell," I mumbled, looking down. And then it hit me.

I spun my stool around so fast I almost gave myself vertigo.

CHAPTER 35

Saki stood in the baby's room, rubbing her belly, head tilted. Suddenly, she felt a kick. "Whoa! Easy tiger," Saki said as she ran her hand around her basketball sized stomach.

Kaylee walked up, and Saki grabbed her hand and put it on her stomach. Kaylee's blue eyes widened as the baby kicked again. "This baby is going to be a soccer player or into MMA like his or her mama." She giggled.

Gretel walked in and put her hand on Saki's shoulder as she walked by. Saki watched Gretel peruse the baby's crib, clothes, and toys.

Saki jumped as her cell phone rang. She looked at the caller ID and answered, "Well, hello, again, Mr. Powers. Your baby is kic—"

"Babe, you have to get out of the house, *now.*

I knew I shouldn't have left." James spoke with a low urgency.

"What are you talking about? You worry too much." Saki watched as Kaylee and Gretel huddled over the crib, gazing at the array of stuffed animals.

Gretel glanced in Saki's direction, gave her a nod and a closed-mouth smile.

"Kaylee and Gretel are here to keep me company. Heidi's on her way from the airport ... and what's that sound. Are you going Co—"

"*Stop!* Yes, I'm going Code 3. Keep smiling and talking but listen to me carefully. "

"Okay." Saki turned away from the pair at the crib.

"Gretel was sent by *them*. She's a mole. You and Kaylee have to get out, *now!*"

"What are you talking about?" Saki's heart pounded faster. "Silly man. We have plenty of swatches here," she said with a shaky laugh.

"Good. How many are in the house?" he asked.

"Only one, honey," she said. "You get to choose only *one* color."

"I can't reach the other agents, but more are on the way. I'm twenty out. And I can't contact the security gate. She probably disabled their phone system."

"What color would you like?" She turned back to the ladies and smiled. "Well, we don't have it here."

"Damn. You left your gun in my vehicle. Do you remember where I hid my mother's back-up Sig?"

"Of course, any color you want is fine." Saki wrinkled her nose and pulled the phone away from her ear. "Kaylee, we have to go to the paint store. *Somebody* is changing their minds about the color," Saki said, nodding to every other word and rolling her eyes, slapping her forehead. Trying to act like the ditzy blonde she was not. "Now he wants *Violet.*" She shot a glance to Kaylee. She'd hoped Kaylee would remember the family safe word.

Kaylee's eyes widened, and she gave a nod of understanding.

Saki frowned as Gretel leaned in closer, as if she were eavesdropping on her conversation. She pulled away from Gretel and headed for the door.

"Saki, I'm hitting a bad cell area. May lose you. Hold ti—" The phone went dead.

Saki continued holding the phone to her ear as she stood on the door's threshold, Kaylee right behind her.

But Gretel snaked a step ahead and blocked the door. She grabbed Saki's phone. "Your husband figured it out, didn't he? That's what I always admired about him. He's a smart agent and will be going places," she said. "You two, on the other hand, are going with me." She pulled out her weapon from the low of her back and drew on them.

"What are you talking about?" Kaylee said. "You heard my sister. James wants a *different* paint color." Kaylee stood in front of Saki, shielding her from the mad woman.

Gretel pushed Kaylee onto the floor. "You

can leave with me or the M.E., your choice. Now move it." Gretel waved her pistol toward the door. "My van is out front."

As Saki walked into the living room, she looked out the window and spotted the leg of a lifeless body protruding from the shrubs. She closed her eyes and bit her lip as it hit her. Saki doubled over and threw her hands on her knees, holding her stomach. "Oh, my God. I got contractions. I need to lie down," she said.

Gretel yanked her by the arm. "I don't think so, Princess. You're not due for a couple more months. There's plenty of room in my van to stretch out," she said.

"I'm due next month," Saki said to Kaylee and scrunched her nose. "We kinda fibbed to everyone. Didn't want anyone thinking we got married because I was knocked up." She returned her attention to Gretel. "So ... you see, this baby can pop out anytime ... Bitch!" Saki furrowed her brows, put her fists to her wide hips and waggled her head like a bobble doll. "Oopsie, I wasn't supposed to swear. Where is my swear jar?" She peered around, looking for anything to disable Gretel.

Gretel shoved her. "Nice try, blondie. Get your asses to the van ... *now*. Or the doc gets it first." She raised the pistol to Kaylee's head.

Kaylee quivered as she stared at Saki. The last time Saki saw that fearful look was a few months ago, when they woke with a dead guy in the root cellar in Montana.

Saki's eyes widened, and she quickly darted her gaze around the room. "I ... I have to pee," she blurted.

"Nice try!" Gretel shoved Kaylee out the door with the gun at her head.

"I'm serious," Saki said. "Do you want to test the bladder of a *very* pregnant woman?"

Gretel shook her head and pursed her lips. "I want her to check it out first." She pushed Kaylee inside the powder room and ordered her to open all cabinets. Kaylee flung open the doors.

"See, nothing there, now can I pee?" Saki gave a little hop to emphasize the urgency of the situation.

"Not so fast ... under the sink." Gretel gestured with the gun.

Sweat poured down Saki's brow. She bit her nails as Kaylee opened the vanity's doors.

Saki bolted inside, shut the cabinet, and pushed them out. "Nothing! Now will you get the fuck out, so I can go!" She put her hands to her belly and looked down. "Sorry, baby. Mama owes you a ton of money," she said as she glared at Gretel, slamming the door in her face. Saki locked the door and turned on the faucet.

"Why do you need the water on?" Gretel barked. "I thought you had to use the bathroom."

"It helps me go, if it's any business to you." Saki growled back. She delicately opened the cabinet door under the sink and removed its contents of cleanser, Windex, extra toilet paper, and so on.

She heard a knock. "Hurry or I'm taking you out, finished or not," Gretel yelled.

"Um … it turned into number two," Saki said, flushing the toilet. She removed the bottom shelf and grabbed the Sig Sauer 9mm and stuffed it in the lower back of her pink maternity capris. Saki flushed the toilet again as she rapidly put everything back. She stood, turned off the water, and flung the door wide, glaring at Gretel.

Just as Gretel turned and pushed Kaylee to the front door, Saki pulled out her Sig.

Gretel flipped back to Saki, pointing her gun. *Pop … pop … pop.*

CHAPTER 36

Kevin O'Malley stood in the back of the bar and made his way over to me. His deep-set, sea-green eyes, and black hair with a dash of salt made my heart flutter. Kevin was six feet and some change and roughly one hundred sixty pounds of lean manliness. When I first met him, Kevin bore a striking resemblance to my late husband, Bradley. But now, he's just Kevin and any similarities have waned.

He wrapped his arms around me and gave me a warm, long embrace.

I nuzzled into the crook of his neck and drew a deep breath. Kevin smelled like some after shave delight that made my eyes roll back. I quickly pulled away when I realized the embrace was longer than my comfort zone.

Sue Dog wiggled her way in between us. She looked at Kevin with what appeared to be an approving gaze. I could tell she instantly liked him.

"A friend of yours?" he asked.

"Long story. Her name is Sue Dog," I said.

"Sue ... Dog? Like in your friend, Sue?" He furrowed his brows.

"Don't ask, another novel," I said, shaking my head. "Although calling her Dog sounds redundant, haven't thought that far ahead ... anyway, what are you doing here?" I scanned him. He wore khaki 5.11 pants, black FBI embossed logo polo shirt, tactical boots. "You're not dressed for a wedding ... hmm." I squinted.

He gestured for me to join him at a table in the back.

Elly May approached us. She grinned and set my unfinished drink down. I gave her a smile of gratitude in return.

"You mind telling me what the hell is going on? You've had quite the day," he said.

"It's been a few months since anyone's tried to kill me. I guess I was due." I sipped my drink and rubbed my arm.

"Not funny, Red," he said, reaching for my hand.

I pulled away. "Sorry, trouble follows me, and people die when they get too close."

"Red, that's for me to decide, isn't it?"

"Wait, how the hell did you find me?"

He pursed his lips. "Always changing the subject ... and your grandma."

"Should've known." I rolled my eyes.

Kevin's head tipped back and just as he opened his mouth to reply, Sue Dog trotted over and put her paw on my lap.

I was scratching behind her ear when a thought occurred to me. "You didn't check your voicemail, did you?"

"I was out of range earlier." He drew a cell out of his cargo pocket.

"No need to now." I leaned over the table, "I saw Max."

"*What*?! You could've led with that," Kevin said.

"There's more." I gave him the detailed account of my afternoon, pulled out my iPhone, and showed him my recon pictures. "I ran the address on my gran ... um, my laptop and it came back to Annaliese Albrecht. The limo out front was blocked, so I did more digging and found it registered to an AA Corp. I've seen that name before but can't place it."

Kevin looked around and tugged my chair closer to his.

"What the hell?" My body tingled.

He leaned in and whispered. "Do you remember in Montana when your grandmother showed us the names under one of the Falcon paintings? The shell companies?"

"Oh my God!" I reared my head. "I suspected the armed men were watching someone," I said. "I'll bet they have both Max *and* my father." I pushed back from the table and stood. "We have to rescue them."

Kevin stood, biting his lip.

"Okay, O'Malley. You and James do the same lip biting thing, spill it."

He shot his eyes wide at me. "You have no idea who this is."

"And you're gonna tell me, right?" I said.

"His name is Stanley James Albrecht-Cordova, SJ for short. His mother is American-German, his father from Mexico. He takes after his father and is the middleman in a Mexican cartel. Think about it. We have reason to believe he hired Chena Fin, the woman in this picture, to facilitate Max's escape from custody. He led them to your father. You need to stand down on this one. You do not want to mess with these people, Rose."

The injustice of it all threatened to choke me. "They messed with me first. They took away my job, my home, my father. They killed my friends. Now I'm a walking dead woman. I've got nothing to lose!" I said.

"Don't be stubborn. You have people who care and love you."

"Love is a four-letter word I can't afford to hear right now." I glared and gritted my teeth. "They can do whatever the freak they want with Max. But they're messing with Teddy Reagan and his daughters."

"I thought you were O'Brien?"

"We had to change names when we were kids. You know all that." I paced and ran my fingers through my hair, adjusting my ponytail. "They're doing God knows what to him." I stopped and stared at Kevin. Tears came out of nowhere and poured down my cheeks. I turned away. I couldn't let anyone, let alone Kevin O'Malley, see me weak and crying.

"We will get him back," Kevin said softly. He cradled my face in his hands and wiped my tears with his thumbs. "I don't understand why SJ would risk coming to the states. He has too many warrants. Like Max."

I cleared my throat and reached for a napkin to swipe at my face. "I saw a hospice vehicle parked out front. I don't know about you, but if your mother was dying, and it's this close to Mother's Day, where would you be?"

"Holy cow! We saw the mortuary van leaving. We thought it was a ruse. You're a genius. He's on the move, gotta go." Kevin grabbed my face and planted one right on my lips. Not a tonguey kiss, just a smooch. He put cash on the table. "The drinks and food are on me. Oh, and send me the pictures, please." He turned and jetted for the front door. He looked over his shoulder and pointed at me. "Stand down, O'Brien. I mean it," he said.

I watched him walk out of the bar. I'd never noticed how great his butt looked. I shook my head and slapped my face. "Snap out of it," I mumbled.

"Ahem." A female voice cleared her throat.

I turned.

Copper stood with her fists planted on her hips.

CHAPTER 37

James's heart pounded out of his chest as he turned the corner to his house. Miami Beach Police Department patrol cars lined the curb, along with swarms of FBI agents going in and out the front door and the backyard. He braked his Chevy Tahoe to an abrupt stop in the driveway behind two paramedics and jumped out. Yellow crime scene tape cordoned off his front lawn. He flashed his badge, ducked under the tape and bolted into the house. He immediately spotted Saki sitting on a stretcher. A paramedic attended to her. Tears welled in his eyes as he dropped to his knees.

"We're okay, honey. They're checking my vitals," Saki said with a smile. "But I tell ya, I owe the baby a lot of money."

James squeezed his wife, kissing her forehead, nose, cheeks and finally her lips. "It's a good thing you put a blank check in the swear jar." He let out a sigh of relief.

Saki pulled away. "Easy, honey. I might pop him or her out like a Pillsbury Dough Croissant Roll," she said.

He sat next to Saki, their foreheads touching. Then he spotted Gretel across the room on another stretcher, handcuffed. A paramedic was wheeling her out of the house.

James jumped to his feet. "I'll be right back," he said, his voice stone cold. He marched to Gretel, who had two officers and an FBI agent around her. As he bent down, he felt as if red hot molten veins protruded from his face and neck. "*You* ... you're a disgrace to this department." He was inches from her face. "If you were a man, I'd beat the shit out of you. And no one would dare stop me," he shouted, gazing at the other law enforcement officers.

Gretel squinted her dark hazel eyes, shrugged and turned her head. She pressed her lips into a thin line.

"You're lucky it's not worse." He motioned to her arm, bound with gauze.

"Sorry, honey, I'll do better next time," Saki called from her stretcher. "And another thing," she said, rolling side to side to a sitting position. "If I weren't as big as a freaking whale and carrying our baby, I would've drop-kicked her as—uh, hinny from here to freaking Cuba." She crumpled her nose and pointed to Gretel.

Kaylee emerged from the powder room.

"Blood pressure, sis," she said, easing Saki back onto her stretcher.

James winked at his brave wife. "You did great, babe," James said as he turned back to Gretel, glaring a hole through her. "I prefer the traitor alive. She's going to have fun in federal prison."

"Sir, we need to transport her to the ER," a paramedic said to James.

"Give me a minute with her," James said.

An FBI agent put his hand to James's chest. "Don't cross the line, Powers."

James snarled and batted his hand away. "My line's at a different level than yours," he said.

"Who. Do. You. Work. For?" James asked slowly and deliberately.

"Lawyer," Gretel replied in kind.

He looked around the room and squeezed her wounded arm.

Gretel winced, glared, and pursed her lips. "They can get to me, my family, anytime, anywhere ... and yours, too." She turned her head. "Lawyer!"

CHAPTER 38

"**Y**a care to tell me what that kiss was about?" Copper asked.

I shot her a look.

"Whoa, what's with the face?"

"Is my face talking again?" I crumpled my nose. "It's nothing. We're just friends," I said.

"Riight. My friends don't kiss me that way. And the way he looks at ya, he has it bad," Copper said. "Besides, your face is red."

I felt my cheeks and cleared my throat. "Anyway, are we ready?" I asked.

Copper motioned for me to follow her to the room with *Private* posted on the door.

I gave Copper a summary of my discoveries, omitting the privileged information Kevin told me.

"Wait." She stopped. "Chatter has it, they

moved Teddy."

"Chatter? Would *you* like to elaborate?" I squinted.

"Can't until we have confirmation. Our intel guy, Rio, is on it."

My stomach churned. Should I tell O'Malley? I considered as we made our way through the door.

"Right now, it's just a quick meet and greet until we get a solid ops plan and more intel."

I was not good with the waiting game, especially with my father's life hanging in the balance. The father who'd been dead to me most of my life and only restored to me a few short months ago. I couldn't think about losing him all over again.

The private room was cozy with dark paneling and a black leather sofa. Five bar stools lined the wall and all but one was occupied. The men sat with their backs firmly pressed against the wall. I estimated the guys' ages varied from early thirties to mid-forties.

Cigar smoke wafted in the air. I gave a little cough and waved my hand. I sucked it up because I didn't want to seem like a wuss.

The second Copper closed the door, conversations stopped, and the room went still. Four sets of eyes were on me.

Sue Dog must've felt my apprehension. She stood at attention between my legs. I felt her little body quiver.

"Hey, guys. This is Rose O' Brien. Ya know her granny, the infamous 'Lily Roo,'" Copper said loudly.

They said "Ah" in unison and returned to their side conversations.

I let out some air and leaned into Copper, and whispered, "She doesn't like to be called, 'Granny.'"

"Noted. Anyhoo ... that went well," Copper murmured.

"Where are Titos and Vino?" I asked, scanning the room.

"They figured since you've met, they didn't need to be here. Besides, they wanted *sushi*." She pursed her lips.

"I never thought of them as sushi guys," I said. "But whatever."

"They'll join our briefing later." Copper nodded to the men. "First on the introduction list is Master Sergeant BoBo. He is the tactical commander and will be leading the operation."

"BoBo ...?"

"No last names, remember?" Copper replied.

"Copy."

BoBo was seated furthest from the door. He was ground zero for the cigar smoke. He set down his stogie and stood when we approached. He was roughly in his mid-forties, about six feet, salt and pepper hair, mostly salt. He wore a black baseball cap, cowboy boots, and jeans. I'd imagined if he wasn't on a bike, he would've had a cowboy hat.

"Charmed," BoBo said. "We all owe your grandma our lives. Any friend of hers is a friend of ours." He tipped his cap and gave me a firm handshake. His brown eyes with a hint of amber disappeared with his smile.

I grinned back as we continued our introductions.

Next was the curmudgeon from the bar.

"This is Rio," Copper said.

Rio stared me up and down but didn't stand. He met my height sitting, so he wasn't tall. But he was stocky and probably could take care of his own. He crossed his arms and grunted. When God was handing out personalities, Rio missed that line.

"Rio isn't much of a talker. His vocabulary consists of maybe ten words, usually with four letters. He mostly grunts and nods, seldom a smile," Copper said.

"I see." I returned his body scan.

"Rio's been gone a while. We're glad he could join us last minute," Copper said.

There was something fishy about him. Sue Dog must've felt the same as her hackles remained at attention. She sniffed around him with a low growl. Like Grandma always said, "You can't fool a dog, they know who to trust." I should've heeded her warning.

Rio had a hardness to him, like someone who'd done time. He'd removed his jacket from earlier and wore a black fitted T-shirt with a skull and crossbones on the front. His arms were sleeved in tattoos. He had dingy brown hair, dark deep brown eyes, premature wrinkles lined his face. He turned his head, and I spotted a diamond stud in his left ear.

"Rio is the best intel officer we've got. Not to mention explosives expert," Copper added.

"I'm the best there is." His voice was as surly

as his appearance. He stood and exited the bar.

"Okay," I said under my breath as we continued down the line of barstools.

"Next, we have Walter." Walter gave me a genuine grin.

"Walter is a nice guy ... until he's not," Copper said. "You don't want to see a pissed Walter. It ain't pretty. But he saved my ass." She patted her prosthetic.

Walter was six feet, three inches, with deep blue eyes, and wavy, shoulder-length jet-black hair. He resembled Max, but with a longer mane and stronger jawline. My mind drifted to what the cartel were doing to him.

I shook it off. Walter was a handsome gent and looked as if he could be on the cover of GQ or Men's Fitness. He had a hard body and obviously took care of himself.

Walter stood and towered over me. He gently took my hand and kissed it. "Has anyone told you how beautiful you are? Are you single? Bec—"

I pulled my hand back and giggled like a schoolgirl, to my own surprise. I rarely fell for the tall, dark, and extremely handsome type. He was Prince Charming on steroids. I felt my face, and it was hot again. He actually made me blush. What the hell?

Copper gave Walter a playful slug. "Walter's a dog," she said with a laugh.

"Next is Si—" Copper did not complete her introductions.

"My name is Simon Rae," the gent said. "Please to meet you, ma'am." Simon Rae stood six feet, four inches and was pure muscle. He had crew-cut brownish auburn hair mixed with a touch of black. And lashes to die for. His brown eyes crinkled in the corners when he smiled. He greeted me with a bear hug, swooping me off my feet.

I let out a tiny, pained squeal as he had a hold of my bad arm. I looked beyond him to Copper for help.

"Easy, tiger." Copper laughed and pulled us apart. "He is a cowboy from Montana. And until a week ago has been working on a cattle ranch."

Simon Rae wore a Gomer Pyle-grin with a dimpled chin and was as sweet as he was goofy.

I leaned in and whispered to Copper, "Does your team only consist of hotties?"

"I never noti—"

My phone buzzed. A text message from James. *Felicity, we are code 4 ... sisters are safe.*

CHAPTER 39

Chena stood at the window and watched SJ slither into the back seat of his Escalade limo with his entourage. "Bloody coward. Leaving me to do his dirty work." She turned to Bruno. "Are they loaded in the first boat? We need to move out. My source tells me the feds will arrive shortly."

"Black Heart and the big bald dude just left in SJ's Bayliner. They're taking Max and Teddy to the other side," Bruno said.

"Excellent." She looked at her watch. "It's seven and I haven't heard from Gretel. Her surveillance cameras are offline, too. That means one thing." Chena smoothed her suit. "You know who to call."

"On it." Bruno grabbed the phone from his side pocket and stepped into the hall.

Chena walked into the downstairs guestroom, picked up her overnight bag, and shrugged into her Armani. As she headed for the back door, Bruno was on her heels.

"You were right. She's in a Miami hospital having a bullet removed. The pregnant one shot her. I got it handled. But we need to move fast. Feds are closer than we think."

"Very good," Chena said calmly as she strode down the boat ramp where Archer waited. He assisted her with her bag onto the idling Chris Craft wooden cabin cruiser. Just as they motored off, Chena spotted blacked-out SUVs swarm the mansion.

"Kill the lights, Archer," Chena said as she crouched below deck. "Get down, all of you."

Archer did as ordered. He quickly motored them out of sight. The half-moon glistening off the lake provided a guiding light.

Chena watched as Archer and Bruno shot wide-eyed glances at each other and back to her. For the first time, she felt panic. Her heart pounded through her ribcage. She peeked her head up and gazed as the mansion grew smaller. She exhaled a loud whoosh and lowered her shoulders. "I think we're in the clear." She sat tall on the seat behind the windshield and buttoned her jacket.

Her phone buzzed. "Status?" she answered it on speaker.

"Still on target." A man with the gruff voice responded.

"Very good. Do they know Teddy is being moved?"

"Affirmative. I'm gonna need two other men for tonight."

"I can spare a couple. Where should they meet you?"

"I'll pick 'em up at the boat dock in thirty."

"We need forty-five," Chena said.

"Copy ... hey gotta go, someone's coming." Click. The man disconnected.

CHAPTER 40

I told Copper to send me the location of our late-night rendezvous and excused myself from her and the team. I quickly dialed.

"What the hell, James. When were they *not* safe?" It was quieter in my brain.

"Hello to you too. And no beloved *AP?* I can say the same thing for you ... *sis*. When were you going to tell me about your day?" James snapped back.

I pulled the phone away from my ear and let out a heavy sigh. "I'm sorry, AP." I gave him the blow by blow, including my run in with Titos. "We're waiting for confirmation of my father's location."

Silence fell on the line.

"Are you there?" I asked.

"I'm processing," he coldly replied.

I imagined James doing the, *what were you thinking*, big bro routine of walking around in circles with his hands on his head.

"Your turn," I said.

He briefed me on the activities in Florida. "So, tell me again how you're going Jane Wayne into the cartel den? Isn't that O'Malley's jurisdiction?"

"Yes. But we have intel they're moving my father. O'Malley's got his line on the big fish, SJ." I squinted at the phone and bit my lip, as if he could see me. "I shouldn't have told you."

"I don't like this one bit. There's nothing I can do from here," James said. "And we're on the move again. We don't know how many moles are inside. But the most recent rat never woke from surgery. We're wheels up in ten. Your Uncle Tubbs is flying us to the Secret Squirrel's *lair*."

What James couldn't say over the phone is they were going to Grandma Lil's in Montana. "Good plan." I paused. "AP ... I know you have a lot on your plate, but ... with your connections in Sacramento, can you *please* have someone sit on my house? I don't want any looters," I begged.

"Felicity, I'm one step ahead of you, love."

For a moment, I felt like we were back in our old goofy Austin Powers routine. James was the AP to my Felicity. How I missed those days. With a heavy sigh, I disconnected and lowered my shoulders. I knew I could count on him.

I peered at Sue Dog and noted she was in protection mode as we exited the bar. Her hackles were high.

The second I stepped outside, the crisp scent of pine trees lingered in the Lake Tahoe air. A sudden icy chill sliced through me. It's been said the weather in Tahoe is so unpredictable one can experience all four seasons in a single day. Just as I threw the hood over my head and zipped my sweatshirt, I spotted Rio loitering around my vehicle, talking on a cell phone.

He had a cigarette hanging off his lip. When he saw me, he ended the call.

"See you at o'dark thirty," he said, as he blew out rings of smoke, poking his finger through them.

I grunted and studied him as I slunk behind the wheel. There was something wrong with Rio. Even Sue Dog had her eyes trained on him with a growl, her fur still on end. But if Copper vouched for him, how bad could he be?

As I left, the sun was sinking low in the sky. It was a clear half-moon night, but there was an eeriness in the air. I couldn't put my finger on it. I was questioning the entire operation. My Spidey senses told me so.

CHAPTER 41

Time was ticking and I grew impatient. I had the urge to drive by the Incline Village mansion, but it instantly passed. The feds were probably there and SJ's people had moved my father and Max. I opted to return to the safe house and prepare. It was a fifteen-minute drive to the cabin. When I stepped inside, the heat blasted my hair back. I'd forgotten I left it on, so I broke another protocol and opened the windows.

It was close to eight-thirty by the time I loaded the Jeep with my gear, except for my Maxim PDX AR15 pistol. I left it on the table for some last-minute adjustments. I snatched the computer out of the fortified room and spotted my helmet with the night vision goggles. I contemplated and decided to grab it.

After fiddling with my AR, I turned on the lamp with the antler shade, melted into the leather sofa and flipped open the laptop. My eyes grew heavy as I watched my father's video a few times. Sue Dog snored away on the couch at my feet, and I too must've dozed off.

I stood on green, thick grass overlooking the ocean, a warm breeze blowing in my long hair. I was young, maybe six years old. Dad was teaching me to kick box.

"Come on Rosie, show Daddy what superheroes are really made of," he said.

As I turned to deliver a round house, my father vanished and so did the ocean. Instead, I stood in a gymnasium, furiously snapping and jabbing at a punching bag. Bradley was on the receiving end, holding it. He let out an "oof" as I gave the bag all I had. Knocking him back with every blow.

"Hey babe, I wasn't cut out for this. I'm a prosecutor. I fight for justice in the court room." He laughed and drew closer.

I closed my eyes and he kissed me. When I opened them, a bright light blinded me. I threw my hands up to shield my face, but my mother was there. She pulled Bradley's hand, and they drew away from me.

"Please don't go," I mumbled.

"I will be watching." A familiar voice resonated. It was not Bradley's, but my father's.

"Whoa." I shot my eyes open. My father's video was on loop and replaying. "I will be *watching*." I rubbed my face. My father's voice echoed again. It hit me. I bolted upright and played it back, but this time I lowered the speed and stopped at the watch. I enlarged the screen.

I set the laptop on the desk, took off my father's black watch and played with the straps, pushing and pulling on anything that would move. Suddenly, there it was. "Oh my God." I squealed like an excited child.

Sue Dog popped her head up, Kelpie ears at attention.

"I can't believe I didn't see this," I said. "This is one of those spy watches." I pushed into the watch case on the right side under the crown. A USB flash drive popped out. It was flush with the contours. I inserted it in the computer, but it required a password. I closed my eyes and tapped my forehead. "It can't be that easy," I mumbled as I typed in, Violet.

Suddenly, encrypted data generated, all flashing before me. I fumbled in my pocket for my phone and dialed Grandma, hoping she was back online.

"Hi, I was just about to cal—" she answered.

"I got it!" I shrieked again.

"I have something for you, too. But go ahead."

I stared at the computer. "Data is popping up on the screen. Holy cow. Remember the shell companies listed under one of the Falcons? Well, their true identities are right here. Stanley James, Max Ryan, and ..." I gasped and covered my mouth.

"And?" she urged.

"Uh ... politicians and a few others I don't

recognize. Along with Social Security numbers. It's all here, money laundering, offshore accounts in the Cayman Islands, wire transfers, pay offs."

"Do you see routing numbers?" Grandma's voice went up a note.

"No, but I believe this is one of two." I furrowed my brows and bit my lip. "Wait, a sec. Teddy, or uh, er, Dad ..." Referring to my father as Teddy no longer felt right. "Was recently at the cabin ... did you know he stayed here?" I spun like a hamster on a wheel. I snatched the laptop bag and felt along the lining.

"Yes, that is a sto—"

"I know. A story for another day." I rolled my eyes.

"I heard the eye roll," she said.

"Of course, you did ... but there are four other hidden watches, all the same." I pulled one out and inserted the USB drive. "Hmm. The second one is blank." I ejected it and tried the third and fourth. They were the same. "I don't understand. Maybe he doesn't have all the information. No routing numbers."

"Granddaughter, what you have may stop the funding of another terrorist attack. You know, the head of the snake. And potentially implicate a corrupt politician or two," she said.

"All funded by cartel. Hey, why is Max's name on here?"

"Remember, he's just a pawn. They used him to find your father."

Anger swelled as I removed the last USB. I placed the other four hidden watches in the side pouch of the computer bag, along with the laptop and set it on the floor.

"Sorry, your buddy Maxwell is in on it."

"Gran, very funny, *not* my buddy." I did some neck rolls and noticed a note pad sitting on the desk. The paper bore indentations as if something were written on the top sheet before it was torn away. "Wait just a moment," I said.

"Another USB?" she asked.

"No, a note pad." I removed a pencil from the drawer and carefully scratched the top sheet. It revealed numbers followed by dashes. "Routing numbers!" I smiled widely. "He must've not had time to put them on a drive ... hold on. I saw a folder in the computer named 'Violet,'" I said.

"Wonderful," Grandma said.

"It is." I bent to retrieve the laptop from the bag and noticed Sue Dog stood at attention, her hackles up, baring her teeth.

Suddenly, the driveway alarm sounded.

"Stand by," I said, snapping my head in the direction of the CCTV monitor. "Do you see this? I think the imps are here."

"Yes, I have the cabin on one of my screens," Grandma said.

I set the phone down with it still on speaker. I put on my helmet, flipped down the night vision goggles, and turned off the lamp. I snatched my handgun from the coffee table and dropped to a crawl.

The vehicle drew closer. In the stillness, the only sounds were of my thumping heart and icy dirt crushing beneath my unwelcomed visitor's tires. Their doors opened but did not close. They surged toward the cabin. I'd forgotten the windows were still open.

"Gran ... lock it all down, no—" I shouted.

RAT-A-TAT-TAT ... RAT-A-TAT-TAT.

CHAPTER 42

Windows blew out as shards of glass sailed through the air. I ducked behind the couch and jammed the gun in the small of my back. I grabbed the laptop bag and yanked Sue Dog by the bandana. Her little body furiously trembled under my grasp.

I couldn't reach the control button to close the bullet-proof window panels in time and hoped Grandma could on her end. So, I moved to Plan B. I pushed the couch over on its side and pulled back the rug to reveal a hidden floorboard. I popped it open, grabbed my extra ballistic vest, and shoved the laptop along with Sue Dog inside for safekeeping. It was roomy enough for a full-grown adult, but I wasn't planning on hiding. I raised my hand to her, ordering her to stay, and secured the board. I dropped and rolled over to the table, snatching the AR.

My safe house instantly became a scene out of the *Godfather* as the bad guys continued to spray the cabin with what appeared to be .223 rounds. Gunpowder filled the room. I slipped on my ballistic vest and watched them close in on the CCTV. There were three of them. They wore black ski masks and helmets with night vision goggles, similar to mine. They were dressed all in dark clothing. I couldn't understand why SJ didn't send the whole damn cartel.

It went eerily silent as I waited for more gunfire. My heart pounded through my sternum. When suddenly I heard branches rustling outside. One tried the door on the porch. He peppered it, but it was fortified. He then put a boot to it. No luck.

Just then, one of the front and the north side window barriers closed. Grandma must have been able to activate them from her end. But the second one up front was jammed open.

I eased into a standing position. The heat seared through my leg and arm. Had I been shot? I couldn't tell. The adrenaline kicked in as more rounds blasted through the only opened window. As I moved, the floor creaked with each step. I made my way to the front door and took cover. I continued to monitor the CCTV and watched one of the men go around back looking for a way in. He would not find it. The second intruder was on the south side of the cabin. Again, no way in.

The third bloke was on the deck. I heard glass breaking beneath his boot. He jostled the bars with his ginormous gloved hands. That's when I unloaded on him. Since they were all wearing body armor, I pulled out my 9mm and popped him in the head. He went down. The other two hustled to the front. They never had a chance to return fire before I blasted them with my AR.

One of them shouted, "Fuck" as he dropped to the ground, clutching his leg. He was lucky I missed his head.

The last man standing was not tall but made up for it in strength. He scooped the wounded guy and dragged him to the vehicle.

I leaned out the window and sprayed them. By the looks of it, I hit the wounded man again. I missed the shorter one as he took cover behind his vehicle's engine block. As he retreated backwards down my driveway, I continued to return fire. It was my turn to blow out his windshield and turn his hood into a holey chunk of metal.

The driveway alarm chimed again as they exited. I leaned against the door and clutched my head. My ears were still ringing from earlier but got worse and I couldn't hear myself think. I'd hide ear protection for next time.

I removed my helmet, flipped on the light that, surprisingly, was not damaged and rushed to retrieve the dog. All was quiet down there. I bit my lower lip, held my breath, and squinted as I threw the floorboard wide. The second I opened it, she leaped into my arms. All forty, bony pounds of her. I commenced breathing once I knew she was okay.

"Aww ... baby girl. I am so sorry." She stared at me with frightened brown eyes, body trembling. Sue Dog nuzzled her head in my neck, making loud *roo roo* sounds. "Okay, girl. You're just fine." I let out a pained squeal. "On the other hand, I'm not so good." She backed away as if she understood my need for space, scurried into the kitchen, and started furiously lapping water.

I removed the laptop bag and discovered my cell. It must've dropped out during the commotion, ending the call. I returned the Swiss Cheese sofa to its normal position and plopped down and gingerly slipped off my vest. I texted Grandma I was code 4 and needed to clean up. I mentioned there was a dead guy outside, and I'd call her when I was done. But since she monitored the cabin, Grandma most likely saw him. Fortunately, the LED screen was tucked away in the corner and was unscathed.

As I peered down, I noticed my pants were holey and my leg began burning. A round must've grazed my thigh. I assessed the rest of my body. My face stung, my hands were cut, and blood soaked through my left sweatshirt sleeve where I felt the wound oozing, yet again. I'd say I fared pretty well.

I limped to the bathroom and gazed at myself in the mirror, just a few cuts on my face and shards of glass in my hair. I stripped and took a quick shower, minus the hair wash. After my Montana trip, I took a first aid/trauma course from my new friend and EMT-Paramedic, Teri. I was ready to suture myself if needed.

After I cleaned up, I applied an antibacterial numbing spray to my arm and leg and bandaged both. Thank God my thigh had a mere flesh wound, no stitches needed, phew. But a nice bruise was forming, and my skin smarted. I felt as if someone punched me. I also had a small laceration to my forehead, nothing a band aid wouldn't cover.

While I dressed, I pondered how I was made. Someone must've put a tracker under my Jeep. "Sons-a-bitches, Titos and Vino. The only two missing." I slammed my fists on the sink and the veins in my neck protruded. "They must be working both sides."

CHAPTER 43

T eddy pried open his heavy eyes as his head pounded through his skull. The sixty-watt bulb swinging above slowly came into focus. He'd been drugged again. The jab to the neck was the last thing he remembered and then it was lights out. He shivered as the temperatures dropped, his leather flight jacket no longer cut the Tahoe bite. As he peered through the blur, he discovered his hands were bound in front with zip ties, as were his legs.

As he adjusted his vision, Teddy spied Max lying next to him, also restrained in the same manner. Probably they both had been dosed. Teddy rolled to a sitting position as every inch of his body throbbed. He was thankful his right leg was unscathed. But the left was pulsating and hot. Likely getting infected.

"Sammy ... uh, Max!" Teddy said, nudging the man's foot.

Max stirred. "Wh ... where are we?" he murmured.

Teddy looked around at the paddles, life vests, rafts. "They moved us to a boathouse," he said in a hushed voice.

"I've got a wicked headache," Max said.

"Clearly you've never been drugged. Oh ... right. You only drug *others*." Teddy snarled, as he knew Max was behind his daughters being on the receiving end of a needle.

"So that's how it feels," Max mumbled.

"Yeah." Teddy let out a sigh.

Max also rolled to an upright position. "The irony," he said.

They stared at one another for a spell or two.

"Who would've thought we'd be together, like this?" Teddy broke the silence.

Max glared and did not respond.

"I always liked you when you were a boy. You had a gentleness about you," Teddy said. "How the hell did you end up like this?"

"No thanks to you," Max said.

"I mean dealing with these people," Teddy said.

Max squirmed and furrowed his brows. "Well, *Theodore* ... if you hadn't killed my father, I wouldn't have been raised by an asshole of a stepfather who beat me every other weekend." His voice grew colder. "Who I killed ... they say in self-defense. They sentenced me to juvenile hall."

"Abo—"

"I'm not finished." Max sat tall. "Only to be thrust into SJ's circle. He taught me everything. And again, I would not be *here*, in this God-awful position if you'd just kept your bloody nose out of it," he said with a clenched jaw.

"There's one thing you didn't understand about your father, Max. He was a good man who let greed take over." Teddy's voice was soft. "He was in too deep with the wrong side. I wanted out of the partnership after seeing it. Your dad knew the feds were closing in on him … and …" Teddy lowered his head. "He was going to shoot himself. We wrestled for the gun, and it went off." Teddy sighed.

"What a load of crap," Max said.

"I swear on my daughters' lives. It's the truth. He was like a brother to me." Teddy swallowed hard.

"Why did *you* end up in prison?"

"I had to take the fall. To protect *our* families. Yours and mine. I agreed to help the feds put people away, and the rest is, well … history."

"You gave up your family to be a spy?" Max said.

"A decision I regret. Look at them. Rose is dead … because of me!" Tears surged.

Max adjusted, leaned in, and whispered. "About that … I don't believe she is. When I arrived at SJ's house, there was a commotion outside the gates. One of his goons, Archer, was talking to a woman who sounded like your daughter," Max said. "I'd know her voice anywhere. But she was attempting a fake, country twang." He let out a snicker. "She was terrible."

"That sounds like my Rosie. But ... I don't understand, Max. In the Keys, you targeted the family. All for the Falcon and your sick twisted revenge. And now you are obsessed with her? You even had her husband murdered ... because he found me," Teddy said.

"It's complicated. He wasn't supposed to die, and I wanted revenge ... until I saw her face to face again. I could not kill her. I love her and want to marry her," Max said.

"What?! It makes no sense at all. What's with your obsession with my daughter?"

"It's not an obsession." Max paused. "My mother, you remember her? She loved Rose and told me I needed to marry a person like her. Strong, independent, loyal, and her beauty forever captivated me. I've only loved two women in my life."

"Max. You were children. She was seven, and you were what? Eleven?"

"I've always felt it ... inside. Rose reminds me of my mother. But Mother passed away from a broken heart that *you* caused." Max glared.

"Max, she had a heart condition. Then she married your asshole stepfather."

"He was conniving, and Mother was in a bad way after Father was mur—killed. She was extremely wealthy and hid a substantial amount of her assets and left it all to me. But he didn't know that and tried hard to charm her. Until he didn't. All the times he held me downstairs and beat me, Mother thought I was at a sleepover. He threatened to kill her if I said anything." Max shook his head. "Anyway, Mother approved of Rose."

"I am sorry ... but Max, she meant someone *like* her ... not Rose. She was just a child."

Max cleared his throat. "Unless we get out of here, they're going to kill us after they get what they want. Speaking of ... where is it?"

The door flung wide.

CHAPTER 44

"I'm gonna whack Titos this time, I swear. Pretending to be on *my* side. Grr." I stood in the living room, assessing my grandmother's safe house, feeling anything but safe. It was Coppola meets Tarantino. I shook my head in disgust.

After popping more Tylenol and antibiotics, I placed the laptop in the safe room, restocked my first aid kit, and took yet another ballistic vest, without holes. I grabbed more ammo for my handguns and Maxim PDX AR15 pistol and topped them all off. I put my Kahr 9 in my bra holster and my Glock 9 in my hip holster. I was about to reach for my Hellcat to stuff in my ankle holster, but my lower body was compromised, so I tucked my stiletto knife in my new boot pocket. A lady could never have too many weapons.

As I sealed both doors, the driveway alarm sounded off again. The skin prickled all over my body. I looked at the CCTV and spotted another SUV slowly edge down the driveway. I shot out the back through the garage, ignoring the throbbing in my leg, and stood in the shadows on the front porch with my AR pistol ready. I stumbled over the dead guy and put on my night vision goggles, bracing for another gun fight.

Just as I flipped my rifle's safety off, my phone vibrated. I ignored it. The SUV drew closer. My heart hammered faster. My phone vibrated again and again. I disregarded it and took aim.

The vehicle's door opened and Sue Dog, who'd been standing behind me, began wagging her tail and tapping her feet in excitement. What the hell? It was a good thing I wore my night vision because Lily emerged. Sue Dog must've sensed her positive energy and was excited to see her.

"Lily Cazier! Holy crap are you lucky," I said. "I almost turned you into minced meat." I lowered my shoulders and put the safety on, slinging the rifle by my side.

Lily greeted me with a warm embrace. "Hey, girl. I texted to let you know I was on your road and even had your grandma call."

"That's what she was going to tell me, until we got interrupted," I said, removing my goggles. "You are a sight for sore eyes, but how and what are you doing here? It's not safe." I yanked her toward the house and turned on the rifle's light so she wouldn't stumble.

Lily jumped as we passed the dead guy.

"Yeah, you missed the party." I bent down and pulled off his ski mask, shining my light on his face. The deceased was a bald, white male in his mid-thirties, large build. He looked like one of the henchman that patrolled SJ's. I patted his pockets. They were empty.

Lily was silent as we made our way through the garage and into the cabin.

"I admire what you've done to the place, it's so ... Tarantino," Lily said with a smirk.

"Funny. We think so much alike. So, what brings you here?" I removed my helmet and rifle and placed them on the kitchen table.

"I was going to wait until James, Heidi, and your sisters arrived, but your grandma wanted me to bring you something special, and, uh, well, Saki ..."

"What?" I spun and nausea brewed.

"She had labor pains on the plane ride to Montana. Tubbs landed safely at the Ravalli County Airport and an ambulance was waiting. She's at the hospital now."

I darted to the sink and leaned over, but nothing came out.

Lily came over and patted my back. "You need to take care of yourself. She is fine and in excellent hands."

I stood upright. "Crap on a biscuit," I said with a wrinkled nose.

Lily pursed her lips and blinked.

"I was supposed to be there for her. I

promised ... and two months early?" I said.

"I guess they were further along."

"I thought so—wait!" I squinted. "*You* flew here?"

"I have my pilot's license for plane and chopper." She stood tall and gave me a cheeky grin. "I've been working on it for a couple years and kept it hush hush. I flew out to help you," she said, scanning me. "Looks like I arrived a little too late." She moved a tuft of hair, stuck with dried blood away from my forehead, inspecting the Band-Aid.

I shoved the hair back. "Just flesh wounds," I said. "Impressive, I've always wanted to get my license. I've only jumped out of planes."

As I made my way to the chair, I scanned Lily. She was decked out in black, from her beanie down to her cargo pants. Even her long, black silky hair was pulled tight into a braid. She looked taller than five-four.

"I'm not sure how much help you can be. The team I'm working with don't like anybody in their sandbox." I grabbed my throbbing leg. "Freakin' A ... son of a b—uck." I winced. "On second thought, I'm gonna need a driver," I said with a curled lip.

"Sure ... and son of a buck? Crap on a biscuit?" Lily tilted her head like a curious puppy.

"Yeah, I promised Saki I'd *try* to curtail my cussing ... for the baby." I shrugged.

Just then Sue Dog jumped on Lily and showered her with kisses. "And you need to explain this little girl." She pointed.

I gave Lily the abridged version. "I have an important job for you. If something happens, will you please take her?"

Just as she was about to respond, my burner phone vibrated. I jumped and peered at the caller ID. "Unknown number."

CHAPTER 45

"Speak," I snapped, putting the phone on speaker.

"Well played, Ms. O'Brien. My name is Chena Fin," the woman said.

"I know who you are!" I said.

"You took out a good man tonight and the other has a few holes in him," Chena said.

"Yeah, the dead guy's still on my doorstep. I'll gladly deliver him if you tell me where."

"Nice try," she retorted.

"I'm surprised you only sent *three*." I stood too fast. The room spun and I fell against the wall.

Lily rushed to me, but I waved her away.

"I guess I underestimated you," Chena said.

"Well ... never underestimate Teddy Reagan's daughters."

"I'm learning that, and your pregnant sister did very well, too. I could use a team like you two." Her tone was steady.

"Not on your fucking life," I shouted.

"Well, that didn't last long," Lily said, almost under her breath.

I shot her a side glare. "You didn't call to offer me a job. Where. Is. My. Father?" I asked slowly and deliberately.

"Don't look so smug, Theodore," Chena said.

My heart dropped. She was in the presence of my dad. A twinge of excitement fluttered my body. He was still alive. "Let me talk to him," I said, pacing the kitchen, wincing with every step.

"Not so fast. You have something I want."

"I have no clue what you're talking about ... can you be more specific?" I wandered into the living room and plopped onto the bullet-riddled couch.

"Don't be coy with me. The *watch*. I know you have it."

I looked at the cracked face and pondered.

"Don't do it, Rosie," my father yelled from the other end of the call. "Argh!!" he shouted a blood-curdling scream.

"What are you doing to him?!" A sharp, sweltering pain seared in my chest.

"Tough little daddy's girl. Let's see how tough you are."

Shouts came from the other end again. "That would be the sound of a pipe against your daddy's knee cap. On his good leg too ... oh, so painful. Tsk tsk," Chena said.

Tears welled in my eyes and gushed down my cheeks. I slid to the floor and pulled the phone away from my ears. I couldn't hear his torturous screams any longer. Whatever my father had done, he didn't deserve what they were surely doing to him. He was a good man and was only doing what was best for his country. I knew that now.

Sue Dog trotted over and propped against me, her paw on my foot.

A third scream came from the other end of the call. "That's for killing my man," Chena said.

I drew a deep breath and sucked back my tears. "This is how it's gonna play out. You touch another hair on my father's head and this USB is gonna be in the hands of the feds. And then ... I'm coming for you, you fucking twat bitch." My voice was eerily calm.

Lily stared at me with wide eyes as she was on her cell phone.

"Then give me what I want," Chena said, equally as calmly.

"When and where?" I asked.

"I'll be in touch. I will arrange a meeting time but come sunrise if I don't have it, both men will be dead. And no cops. I watched the feds swarm SJ's house. But it's a shame they didn't find anyone there. He's flying out of South Sh—never mind."

Lily mouthed, *keep talking,* waving her arms at me. I assumed Grandma was tracing the call.

"Wait ... how do I get a hold of yo—"

Click. Chena disconnected.

Lily put the phone on speaker.

"Shoot. Nice try Granddaughter," Grandma said with a shaky voice. I could tell the screams from her son were too much for her too. "I traced the call too late. All I know is she's calling from Glenbrook."

"That's on the East Shore, near Cave Rock," I said. "But, Gran, did you catch that? SJ is taking off from the South Shore ... uh, the Lake Tahoe Airport. Can you relay it to Ke—"

"Already did," Grandma said. "And do you remember what you told me about knowing your purpose? It's time. Bring your dad home. Be careful and watch your six. Oh, and Lily has a piece of equipment for you." Grandma Lil disconnected.

My heart ached for her. Her only son, being tortured within an inch of his life. I stood, wiped my face with my sleeve. My phone buzzed with a text. It was Copper, giving me the meeting location on the South Shore.

It was time to get my dad back!

CHAPTER 46

The "equipment" Grandma mentioned was a state-of-the-art ballistic undershirt. Black, bulletproof, long sleeve. Great for undercover work. Tonight, I was not undercover, but extra protection couldn't hurt.

"It's new. She's had her people refining it. You may still want to wear body armor over it," Lily said.

I squinted. "She's not really retired, is she?"

"From the CIA. But she'll never stop. Eventually, she's gonna need someone to take over the fun stuff."

I gave Lily a side glance.

"Don't look at me. You're the most likely candidate," Lily said.

"What? Rescuing mustangs is not fun

enough?"

"That's not the fun I was talking about."

"I can't think of that now. We gotta roll," I said.

It was just after midnight by the time I battened down the hatches and transferred my gear from my vehicle to Lily's rented Ford Expedition. I'd checked under my Jeep and discovered a tracking device. Figures. Who could be the double-crossing rat? Heck, it could be Copper herself. Anything was possible at this point. And money bests loyalty.

On the forty-five-minute drive to South Shore, I had the urge to call Kevin and let him know what I was doing. But I resisted. His team had already hit SJ's house and hopefully caught up with him before he fled to Mexico.

According to Copper's text, they were in a small cabin off the Pioneer Trail, just behind the casinos. It was close to one a.m. when we veered off Hwy 50, making a right at the D's restaurant.

Lily and I drove through the double arches on the Nevada side of Tahoe. It was a 24-hour town and easy to find something quick to eat. I ordered a double with cheese, no fries and got Sue Dog a double hamburger patty. Lily and I added extra caffeine. I was going to sleep for a week after this ended. Not to mention clean up my diet.

It was one-thirty, and I still had not heard from Chena. Something was amiss. Sue Dog must've felt it too. She whimpered, put her paw on my shoulder, and licked my face.

I turned to Lily. "You promise to take care of her?"

"Of course I will. But we won't let anything happen," Lily said.

We pulled up to the cabin. Blackout shades covered the windows, and it appeared no one was home. It was dark. There were no streetlights. Even the moon was hidden behind the clouds.

"This is the address Copper gave me. Pull around," I said.

There were more vehicles as we made our way to the rear. The only illumination was the cherry off a cigarette. The hair on the nape of my neck stood on end.

Sue Dog let out a low snarl.

CHAPTER 47

The closer I drew, I realized he was the curmudgeon from the bar, Rio. He was dressed in all black from head to toe and was already dirty. But why? Rio was leaning against his silver Toyota Tundra, cigarette hanging out of his mouth and talking on the phone. He disconnected when we arrived. It appeared to be a pattern with him.

Sue Dog approached him with her hackles up, snarling.

"Easy girl. He's on our team," I said, trying to convince myself, too.

We approached the back door, and a light flicked overhead.

Rio jutted to me and scanned Lily from head to toe, grunting as we walked past him.

Lily leaned in. "Nice guy," she whispered.

"Yeah. All good. He's the best at his job ... so they tell me." I looked over my shoulder and considered him for a second or two. He was enigmatic, but why?

Before I had a chance to knock, Copper opened the door and we entered through the kitchen. Sue Dog trotted up to her like a long-lost friend, wagging her tail. Copper bent and greeted the dog with baby talk, then stood and nodded to Lily. Copper's demeanor changed as she put on the same game face I'd seen earlier.

"She's good," I said to Copper. "My grandma vo—"

"Yep. Your gran gave me the 411." She addressed Lily. "I hear you're a pilot?" They shook hands.

"I am," Lily replied with a puffed chest.

"We may need one. Follow me." She motioned to the living room. "Sergeant BoBo is working on the ops plan right now."

Nine sets of eyes examined us as we stepped inside. The entire team, including Mia and Butterfly, were present. I searched the room and noticed Titos was missing. Hmm.

Sue Dog wandered over to Mia, who'd been lying on the couch and gave her smooches. She could be a therapy dog.

I immediately ruled out Copper and Mia as suspect moles since they were dog approved.

I pulled out my phone and glanced at it. No missed calls or texts from Chena.

As Copper made the introductions of the entire team to Lily, I eyed the cabin. It was a cozy, approximately nine-hundred-square-foot

A-Frame, one bedroom and one bath, with a loft. It had a tiny kitchen and no formal dining area. The living room was congested. The couch was pushed to the side with the matching recliner to accommodate the team, their equipment and a giant rolling dry erase board.

While Lily was doing her meet and greet with the team, Copper nodded for me to join her in the kitchen.

"Where is Titos?" I inquired. I grew suspicious. He *had* to be the mole who launched the surprise attack on the cabin. My mind wondered as I peeked at my cell again.

"He's on a food run and does not participate much anymore. He says he's seen enough and leaves it to us now," she said with an eye roll. "Personally, I don't think he wants to mess up his new prosthetics. He has all this money and, for all intents and purposes, is dead. He needs to lie low ... something you *didn't* do." She examined the bandage on my forehead and gestured to my leg. "And, um ... ya wanna explain what the hell happened to you since I last saw you? You're walking as if ya fell off a horse."

My distrust of Copper waned. I gave her the rundown of my evening horror show. Including my suspicions of a traitor amongst her people. I felt my phone vibrate, or so I'd thought. I fished it out of my pocket. Nothing. I let out a heavy sigh.

She leaned in and whispered, "So, ya think one of my team members is a rat?" She crossed her arms and stared. "And do you have someplace better to be? Ya keep lookin' at your damn cell."

"Yes, I do. I mean, not someplace else to be." I stood back and held my arms, too. "But how else would a tracker be on my Jeep?" I asked in an accusatory tone.

She shook her head repeatedly. "No, no, no, no. Impossible." Her hands were behind her neck as she scanned the room.

"To answer your question. Chena called me. So, this ops plan may be for nothing." I nodded to the erase board in the living room. "But something is fishy. I've not heard from her. My grandmother tracked her phone to the East Shore in Glenbrook."

"Rio advised us of the location. So … perhaps Chena is playing ga—"

"Or the feds got her." My voice went up a note. "And perhaps they already rescued my father. I'm gonna call Ke—"

"*No!*" Copper grabbed my phone.

I snatched it back and stuffed it in my rear pocket. "Why not?"

Copper put her leg back, hands on hips, and looked at her shoes. "They have Teddy and Max. Rio did some recon and confirmed it," she said, beckoning me to rejoin her in the living room.

"Wait." I grabbed her arm. "Chena was adamant. She wants to make the exchange with *me*. And she knows the feds are in town. She saw them hit SJ's house. She won't hesitate to kill my father and Max."

Copper looked around the room. "Do they look like feds? We do this our way."

CHAPTER 48

Sergeant BoBo stood front and center with an unlit stogie hanging from his lip. He and the rest of the team were dressed in jeans, sweatshirts, and black tactical boots. I assumed they'd be decked out in camos. Copper said it was a covert, non-sanctioned military operation. Street clothing allowed them to blend in to avoid detection. Get in and get out. But why was Rio in all black?

They had MK18s, M16s, M4s, and other ARs I didn't recognize, rigged with lights and suppressors. Each carried a 9mm. They loaded their ballistic chest rigs with extra mags, radios, knives, and other essential items. Each team member's tactical helmet was equipped with night vision and a headset for communication that was attached to their push to transmit radios. They were ready for their extraction.

BoBo commenced writing on the board. "We hit it at zero three hundred hours. But first we need an extra set of eyes on the house."

I stood with my mouth agape. There were recent photos of Max and my father. It all became surreal. I walked up and snatched one of my father and studied it. My stomach tightened. I drew a deep breath and stood tall. My tear ducts were dry. Now I was in complete rage mode.

"I volunteer," I said in a cold, detached voice.

"I thought you'd say that. But ..." Sergeant BoBo snatched the picture and taped it back on the board. "Under *no* circumstances will you be on the entry team. You are in no shape physically." He looked at my leg, arm, and face. "Or mentally. You are a liability. You will stand down ... Agent O'Brien. Plus, you've never trained with us."

I was speechless, but he was correct. This was his operation, and I was too close to the subject.

"But, I also know your type and you need a job," BoBo said. "So ... agreed. You and Rio will set eyes on the house." He returned to the board. "The entry team will be the usual suspects. Walter, Simon Rae, Cop ..."

I tuned out and shrank to the back of the room as the sergeant commenced with his ops plan.

Titos entered with burgers and fries, smiling

widely at me. He was wearing jeans, a turtleneck sweater, and black western-style boots. There was not a scratch on him. He had a calm demeanor. Damn. I ruled him out as the mole.

Just then, Rio slithered in and stopped next to me. I smelled the cigarette smoke before I saw him. He leaned in. "Looks like it's you and me, *partner*." He raised his brows and stood with a wide stance, fists on hips.

"If you're here, who's got eyes on the house?" I squinted.

"Don't worry, I got it handled!" Rio snapped.

"And ... why are you stuck with me?"

"You ask too many damn questions." He glared and sighed. "I'm the intel guy, remember. Also, I'm the FNG and haven't worked with this team in a while ... I've been gone." Rio said.

"Hmm, I remember those days of being the freaking new guy and it sucked." I stared back. I saw through Rio's attempt at small talk. I caught him staring at my father's watch, so I pulled my sleeve over it. My spidey senses told me to watch my six with him.

"But ... um, first we gotta grab another van. It has all the fun equipment the team doesn't have ... and then some." Rio headed to the door. "Let's roll."

Lily stood on the other side of me. "I guess Sue and I will be on standby?" She threw her arms out. She looked as confused as I was.

"Taking care of my fur baby is the most important job," I said in a loving voice as I dropped to my knees. Sue Dog licked me and stared with her sweet puppy eyes. I felt like it was a permanent goodbye. I fought the tears and cleared my throat. She returned a look of understanding. If she could salute me, she would've.

I stood and Lily gave me a fist bump.

"Go get your father. Sue will be just fine," Lily said.

I turned to Rio. "Let's do this."

CHAPTER 49

It was two-thirty when we left the cabin. I grabbed my jacket, tossed my bag containing the essentials—extra ammo, trauma shooting kit, Bushnell binoculars, leather gloves, and helmet with night vision—in Rio's back seat. I slipped on my ballistic vest and adjusted my tools on my nylon gun belt. I did a press check on my side arm and AR pistol. With all that went down tonight I needed to make sure my rounds were chambered. Check. Ready to rock and roll.

With my AR by my side, I slid in the passenger side of Rio's Tundra, wincing with every move. I looked over and he was staring with a blank look. "What? Stay ready so you don't have to get ready," I said.

"You heard the sarge. We are eyes only," Rio

said.

"And if it goes to the crapper? Where's your gear?"

He nodded to the back. But I saw he had his Glock 9mm on his hip.

"So, where's the van?" I asked.

"The Village parking garage."

That seemed an odd place. "Why there and not at the house?"

"It … uh was being repaired," he said with a heavy sigh.

I could tell my incessant questioning was getting under his skin. A few minutes later we arrived at the underground garage entrance. The gates were up so Rio motored through. Our tires squealed with every turn.

"I've been waiting for this for a long time." He wore a smile for the first time.

"Huh?"

"Uh … this operation," he said.

Something was going on. I was sweating and my pulse rate increased. My anxiety rose to an octane level.

Rio yanked the wheel to the right and parked next to a white panel van, no plates, and no side or rear windows. It was the only vehicle in the garage. As we exited, he loped around to the driver's side and found the van's keys on the floorboard and started it.

I snatched my bag and hustled to the passenger door.

Rio blurted, "Wait … uh … the door is stuck. Go to the back."

I furrowed my brows and gripped my

weapon.

"Uh ... I wanna show you something. It'll knock your socks off," he said, jumping out of the vehicle.

Just as I stepped behind the van, a black town car pulled up, bright lights blinding us.

I threw a hand up to shield my eyes from the glare. "What the hell? That's rude," I said.

The driver idled. No one exited. It hit me and my body stiffened. Chena was in the vehicle and Rio was the snake. That's why she didn't call. It was a sick game. "The only winners at life are those who control the game." I think Meyer Lansky, the former mob accountant, once said that.

I growled as I stepped back, drawing my weapon. But I was too late to the game. I felt a fierce thud at the back of my head.

CHAPTER 50

"It's zero three hundred, where the hell are Rio and Rose?" Copper seethed as she stared at Walter, Simon Rae, and Butterfly sitting elbow to elbow in the rear of the van. They were parked two rural blocks away from the target address. They were rigged up and ready to rumble. Copper grabbed the phone and dialed. "BoBo, have you heard from Rio or Rose?"

"Damn it, I was hoping you did," he replied.

Copper disconnected and called another number and put it on speaker. "Mia. Any contact with Rio or Rose?"

"Negative. Just Lily and Titos ... oh, wait. Lily said they left thirty minutes ago to pick up more equipment?" Mia responded.

"More equipment?! We have all we need ...

standby." Copper grabbed her radio. "Copper to BoBo. We've got a problem. Rio and Rose are MIA. Do we proceed?"

"Have Mia pull up the last known location of his vehicle," BoBo ordered.

"Roger." She turned to her phone. "Mia, did you copy?"

"Affirmative. Uh … we lost the signal. Either it was disabled, or they went underground. Their last known location shows them in front of the Village parking garage."

"Copy. Send Titos to check it out," Copper said to Mia.

Static was heard on the radio. "Rio to Sarge. We are in position. Battery died. We have eyes on the target. The subjects are confirmed inside."

"Roger," BoBo said. "Copper did you read? We are en route."

"Affirmative," Copper replied.

A few moments later, BoBo and Vino pulled up behind Copper's van and flashed the lights.

Copper continued on to the target location. Just as she was two houses down, she shut off the engine. All six team members lined up, flipped down their night vision goggles over their helmets and had weapons ready.

BoBo looked at Copper. "Where the hell is Rio?" he whispered in her ear.

She shrugged.

Bobo shook his head and signaled, one, two, three and gestured his hand to move. All six converged on the cabin. They had trained hundreds of hours, executing their missions, and moved with ease. Walter, Butterfly, and Simon Rae covered the back, while BoBo, Copper, and Vino took the front.

Vino was the breacher and carried an Esty Breaching Ram.

BoBo tried the door first. It was locked. He nodded to Vino.

Vino swung and *BAM* smashed in the front door. Since the team made their presence known, there was no need to be silent. The team broke through the entrance of the eight-hundred-square-foot cabin. BoBo and Copper cleared the front room and bathroom while Vino went through the kitchen.

"Clear, coming out," Vino announced.

That left the bedroom. The door was locked and needed to be cleared for potential threats.

Copper and BoBo looked at one another and shook their heads. Things did not add up for Copper. The cabin was cold and dark. There were no signs of anyone present.

BoBo nodded to Vino.

Vino breached the door.

BOOM!

CHAPTER 51

I was on a cold, hard, metal roller coaster with no cushioned seats, or so it felt. I flickered my eyes until they were at least half opened. I had a pounding headache, immediately followed by nausea as cigarette smoke wafted in the air. Where was I? And then I remembered.

Rio! He'd kidnapped me, hence the retched smoke smell and the panel van. It all came back to me.

I shivered as I glimpsed through the only window in the van, the windshield. It was neither dark nor totally light out. Must be dawn. The sun was rising in the eastern sky. The world was ready to take on another day. A new beginning. My favorite time of the day. Except today, which sucked so far. Although maybe better than yesterday. Hopefully no more friends had been killed yet today.

My brain was fuzzy, but I remembered being hit over the head. I must've been drugged, too. As my vision came into focus, I discovered he handcuffed my wrists in front of me, while my legs were bound with zip ties. I felt along my neck where the worm jabbed me and inspected the cuffs.

What the hell? Disbelief bled into anger. They were pink! With my badge number etched on them. "These are my old cuffs … asshole," I grumbled under my breath. I'd forgotten they were attached to my belt, which was missing, along with my vest, weapons, and my jacket. The jerk didn't have the courtesy to turn on the heater. I was freezing.

I shook my head and rolled to my right. I was staring at two sets of restrained legs. I scanned upward and gasped. Two bodies lay next to me, not moving, and both were bound with zip ties. The one beyond the first had his back to me, but the other, I was facing.

My heart swelled. Although it had been over twenty years, he'd been beaten within an inch of his life, and burn marks covered his body, I knew it was him.

"Daddy," I cried in a low murmur as I inched my way over, caressing his ghastly pale face.

He opened his lids, looked at me and tears surged in his blood-shot blue eyes. "Rose Bud," he said with a weak smile. "Bad time for a reunion." My father's voice was raspy. We cried, squeezing one another's hand. His fingers were a mangled, bloody mess.

I sucked up my tears and rolled to a sitting position. There was blood everywhere, a total crime scene. I nudged the other, who I knew was Max, with my toe. He stirred, rolled over and opened his eyes. I had not been that close to him since he tried to kidnap me in Montana. He only had a swollen jaw, no other scratches. The cruel irony.

The driver turned. "Hello, sleeping beauty," he said with a guttered laugh.

"Screw you, asshole." I snarled.

I turned to my father, who'd never heard me swear and mouthed, *sorry.*

He blinked and gave me a closed-mouth grin.

"Why are you doing this, Rio? For the money?" I looked at Max. "You know Max is loaded. You could've just taken it from him."

Rio didn't reply. He puffed on his cigarette and put the pedal to the metal.

As we careened down the winding highway, the three of us flailed around in the back. We were tossed around like pills in a bottle. I landed on top of Max. Our eyes met, and he shot me a wide smile. He'd changed colognes. It was a good thing as the other was an olfactory nightmare of our time together in Key West.

"Hello, Rosie." Max was wide awake now, with a Cheshire cat grin.

I rolled off him and wriggled again to sit. This time I grabbed the passenger seat head rest and leaned forward.

"Seriously, why are you doing this? You're a traitor to your team."

"Screw them. They ain't my team," Rio said as he extinguished the cigarette in the palm of his hand.

As I peered out the window, I discovered we were on the back side of Kingsbury Grade, headed toward Gardnerville. If I wasn't being driven to my death by a lunatic, I would've enjoyed the breath-taking views of the Carson Valley.

I gripped the seat and realized my father's watch was gone. Chena must've taken it. "Jeezo, sorry I missed meeting Chena. I would've punched the bitch in the face. And you're a bigger bitch for going along with it."

Rio gave me a quick look.

"You got the watch and the money. What do you want from me—from us?"

Rio was silent for a spell. "Revenge," he finally said.

"What?"

"I don't look familiar?"

"Other than the bar? No."

"I'm not surprised. I met you once in the parole office when my nephew was first released from prison. You made *all* these promises to help him and keep him on the straight and narrow."

"What? Who? And I *never* make promises. I only vow to do my job." I seethed through gritted teeth.

"We had high hopes for him. He was my sister's *only* son. She couldn't live without him and drank herself to death. My mother had a heart attack with her only daughter and grandson dead ... because of you all!" he shouted, lighting another cigarette.

"Who the hell are you talking about?" I asked.

"Jessie. Jessie Jones." He blew a puff of smoke in my face.

I coughed and plopped back, putting on my thinking cap. I edged forward again. "How the *hell* is that my fault? I did everything to get him help. I didn't kill him, a sniper did. And ... I'm not sure if you're aware of this, but he murdered my husband!" I shouted so loud Max and my father jumped.

I peeked over my shoulder at Max and returned my gaze to Rio.

"By the way, did you know Max ordered him killed?" I crumpled my nose at throwing Max under the bus. Hell, I did more than that. I ran him over with studded snow tires.

I glanced at Max again. He lowered his gaze. It was the first sign of remorse he'd *ever* shown.

"I knew Max ordered the hit. The sniper is just a paid assassin and trust me will get his in the end." Rio opened the window a crack. "An eye for an eye. I took care of his cousin and the rest of 'em. He'll live with the consequences. But you three are *responsible*," Rio said. "Soo ... ya see, I got three of you for three of my family members. Fair trade, I'd say." He sucked his teeth.

It suddenly occurred to me. "*You* are the

explosives expert. You blew up my house and killed my friend."

"Collateral damage. It was supposed to be you."

I felt gut punched. I fell backward and looked at the two men.

Max wore a far-off stare. My father, on the other hand, needed serious medical attention. He was moaning and his breathing was shallow. My heart sunk. Rio didn't care about the watch or money. He wanted only revenge, which was much more dangerous. There was only one way this was going to end.

CHAPTER 52

"What do you mean, you lost them?" Kevin O'Malley paced the cabin.

"Hey! We almost blew up this morning. Freakin' Rio set us up and wired the door to an explosive device. His *specialty*," Copper shouted. She stood in Kevin's face. Her clothes were torn, and her face covered in lacerations.

Kevin ran his hands through his hair. "I'm sorry. Is everyone okay?" He peered around the empty living room and back to Copper.

"Vino is in the hospital. They may not be able to save his leg." She stroked her prosthetic. "I guess we'll be matching. Sarge and the rest of the team are standing vigil."

Kevin shook his head and blew out a sigh. "I told Rose to stand down and let us handle the situation." He pounded his fists on the back of the chair.

Just then, Lily entered the cabin with Sue Dog on her heels, Titos close behind.

"We found Rio's truck. We traced it to the underground parking garage." Titos said as he ambled to Kevin. "Rose's things were there too, including her cell phones." He set Rose's gear and phones on the couch.

"I'll deal with you later. And why aren't you at the hospital with your cousin and the rest of *your t*eam?!" Kevin said, glaring at Titos.

"I need to keep busy." He let out a heavy sigh. "Ya don't see me ... I'm dead, remember? The deceased don't get arrested. And don't forget your girlfriend and sweet cheeks over here." Titos pointed to Lily. "Kidnapped me." He was in Kevin's face. "So, you deal with me? You deal with them too," Titos's Bronx accent took over his dialect.

Lily snaked in between the two and yanked Kevin by his arm. "This won't help us find Rose and the guys. If you two put your winkies away for now, you can have a measuring contest later."

The two men snarled as they went to opposite sides of the room. Kevin held a grudge against his former co-worker. He never forgave Titos for going rogue. And the news of Rose and Lily kidnapping him was new information Kevin had to process.

Lily picked up her phone and slipped into the kitchen, returning moments later with a laptop. "Okay, Lillian. I have you on speaker."

"Good morning all. Copper, I'm sorry the operation went south. I'm just glad you are all okay. But boy, if I *ever* get my hands on that *monkey punk*, Rio, I'm going to bump him off myself." She let out a heavy sigh. "But for now, we need to find my son and granddaughter."

Lily set the laptop on the coffee table and typed away. She turned the computer around. There was a map on the screen with a moving dot. "Here's what we have so far. Rio is at the top of Kingsbury headed for the Valley," Lily said.

Kevin shuffled over to the computer. "How are you ladies tracking them?"

"I brought Rose a ballistic undershirt. Ms. Lil hid a tracking device in it."

"Does Rose know?" Kevin asked.

"No," Lily said, "but we gotta move. Now. We have access to a chopper."

Kevin grabbed Rose's Maxim PDX AR15 pistol and her extra mags and headed for the door. Just then his phone chirped.

Kevin held his breath and braced himself for a butt chewing.

CHAPTER 53

"Before you yell, how is Saki?" Kevin asked James as he followed Lily, Copper, and Titos in his rented Denali.

"She's hanging in there. The baby's not here yet. They are monitoring her and the baby's vitals. Kaylee and Heidi are in with her now. But, damn, I gotta tell ya. There are words flying out of her mouth I've never heard before. I think she's made up a few," James replied.

"I'm glad they're both okay. But ... boy, your sister-in-law is stubborn as hell. You know that? It's a good thing she's cute." Kevin furrowed his brows.

"Tell me something I don't know. Please find her. I haven't told Saki that Rose has been kidnapped. Not until you locate her. And Kev, none of this is your fault. Oh, before I forget, did you get your big fish?"

"Yep, we intercepted Stanley James at the airport. We called ahead of time and had his plane held up, but Chena Fin and her goons are MIA. I hope the information Teddy discovered is still in the hands of the good guys. We can really use it to nail this son-of-a-bitch and anyone else on that list. But that takes a back seat. Rose is the priority. We're headed to the chopper, hoping to catch up with Rio. I called it in to the locals and the Nevada Highway Patrol. But not knowing the description of his vehicle is challenging. We are following a blip on a screen. And ... I know it's not my jurisdiction, but I ... I can't stand down on this ... I love her."

"I know you do, bro," James said.

Kevin blew out a sigh. "Why do you think I volunteered for all that extra *training* in Sacramento? It was an excuse to see her. And every time we'd meet for lunch or dinner, I fell deeper. You asked me once when it was I first fell in love with your partner. It was last year when she barged into my briefing in Key West. Her vibrance, confidence, and beauty captivated me." Kevin smiled. "She even asked how many times I looked at her photo because it had deep creases. I was so embarrassed, I snatched it from her. I've never told her," Kevin's voice trailed. "Damn it, I can't lose her ... not now." He slammed his hands on the wheel.

"One thing I know about my partner, she's too stubborn to die. She's a resourceful little brat, but she's our brat … hey I gotta go. Kaylee just waved me in. It's time for baby Powers to join the team."

"Congratulations, brother. I wish we could be there."

"Me too. Keep me posted." James disconnected.

Kevin swung his SUV into the Lake Tahoe Airport, snatched the AR, and bolted to the chopper.

"Okay, Lily, let's see what you got," Kevin said.

She smiled and adjusted her headset. "Buckle in and we're wheels up."

CHAPTER 54

I leaned back and pondered our fate. The rear door's handles were wrapped with a heavy chain and padlocked. No getting out that way. That left the sliding door.

"What are you thinking?" My father whispered as he squirmed to an upright position and leaned against the van's back door. "You look like your mother when she was deep in thought." His Adam's apple bobbed as he swallowed. "Rosie, there's not much time. One of my biggest regrets was not being there for you and your sisters."

"Apologize when we get out of this ... but I saw the pictures. I know you were at my wedding, our graduations, every major event," I said in a hushed voice.

My father had tears down his cheeks. "Your

mother's funeral was the hardest. I wanted to comfort you both."

"You were there?"

"Hidden in the shadows and disguised. It was risky, but I had to. She was the love of my life."

"Stop." I held my hand to him. "Let's reminisce later." I needed to keep anger alive in my gut, not pity.

Max was silent.

I scanned the van looking for something to disarm the weasel driving and that's when I felt around for my gun. It was missing from my bra holster. "I hope you copped a good feel, Rio. That's gonna be your last," I said with a snarl.

"I know your type, weapons hidden everywhere," he said.

I threw my head back, closed my eyes, and stretched out my legs. Something poked my ankle, and my eyes flew open. The knife I'd hidden in my boot. Rio wasn't quite as thorough as he believed.

My immediate thought was to cut my bra and use the under wire to take my cuffs off like I trained my sister. No time and not with my father and Max staring at me. Second thought was to just cut Rio's throat, but that would take us flying off the side of the mountain. Not a good plan.

That left my third thought. Keep Rio talking. If I was too quiet, he'd get suspicious.

"So, asshole, where are we going?" I blurted as I covertly slid my hand inside my boot, removing the knife.

"You really need to ask?" Rio snarled.

"I'm curious that way." I slid the action button forward, and the blade automatically released. *Click.* I coughed to cover up the sound.

Whew. He didn't hear it. I cut my legs free. But there was nothing I could do about the handcuffs.

Rio took a quick look over his shoulder. "What the hell are you up to?" The van swerved and we fishtailed.

"I'm checking on my father!" I barked as the knife slipped out of my cold hands and rolled to him. My eyes widened as my dad's boot caught the handle. "Keep your eyes on the freaking road," I shouted.

I inched over to the guys while peeking over my shoulder. I cut my father's wrist and ankle ties. Then Max's wrist zip ties. I handed him the knife. While Max was freeing his legs, I crawled to the front, trying to block the activities in the back.

As I gazed out the front windshield, I knew precisely where we were on the Grade. A turnout was around the corner. I had a flat tire there once and if memory served me correctly, it was approximately a mile long. I hoped it was still there and unoccupied.

I took another quick look back and noted they were both free. I shot glances between the side door and Max and jutted my chin to it. He finally caught on and nodded in return.

I edged closer to Rio. "You know, at this point, all you have are kidnapping charges. It won't get you much time," I said. "But add triple murder? That's another story. You might get the chair." I snorted. I didn't mean it to be a funny snort and it came out rather snarky.

"I'll get time, regardless. I have two strikes already. Ain't got nutin' to lose. I'm gonna do away with all of you and take off with the money." He gestured with his head to the black duffle bag that sat next to the AR15 on the passenger side floorboard. "And live happily ever fucking after," he said with a bark of laughter. "Now shut the hell up and sit back."

I drew my face closer to his. "I'm sure we can work something out. I can get you more money than you ever imaged. Max is über, filthy rich," I whispered in his ear.

"Instead of cuddling with me, ya may wanna spend the remaining time with your *daddy*," he said, yanking his head away.

We rounded the corner and there was the turnout. Here was my chance. I held my breath and got directly behind him. I raised my cuffed hands, braced my legs against the back of his seat, and with the full weight of my body, used the cuffs as a garrote and yanked as hard as I could.

He gurgled and his cigarette fell from his lips. Rio thrashed and slapped at me.

We continued to fishtail left and then a quicker right. The van slowed as his foot left the accelerator. With my hands still around his neck, I wrenched harder and twisted my body. I extended my leg and used my foot to steer us away from plummeting to our death.

Rio went limp and his head fell forward.

"Door … now," I shouted.

"Are you kidding me?" Max yelled.

"Oh, for crying out loud," my father said as he struggled to unlatch the sliding door.

I loosened my death grip just as the side door popped open.

"Jump!"

"No, way," Max yelled back.

"Grab Dad and move," I shouted as the van careened toward the side of the mountain.

Like a linebacker, I hurled my body and rammed my shoulder into Max, shoving him out. He rolled about like a rag doll on the sandy turnout. Seconds before we collided with the mountain, I grabbed hold of my father with my shackled hands and jumped.

CHAPTER 55

My intestines twisted like a pretzel as the three of us were tossed in every direction. Seconds later, the van slammed into the side of the hill and flames soon engulfed it. I crawled onto my hands and knees, making my way to a stand, or in my case, a stagger. Adrenaline coursed through me. I ignored what was surely broken bones or at least sprained joints and refused to surrender to the lightning bolt of pain that seared through my body.

Nothing could stop me from reaching my father.

"Dad ... daddy!" I cried as his motionless body lay a few feet away. I moved as quick as I could, dragging my leg, leaving trails of blood in the sand. It didn't matter. All that mattered was my father. The years of resentment liquified in the scorching van.

I collapsed next to him, checking for a pulse. Nothing. I placed my ear to his mouth. Still nothing. I shook him. "Dad? Dad ... Teddy Reagan, wake your ass up!" I shouted as tears cascaded down my face. My heart stopped and I couldn't catch my breath.

Max joined me and put his hand on my shoulders. I allowed it for the moment.

I began CPR when my father opened his eyes and mumbled something.

"Daddy?" I shrieked.

We embraced, and both cried.

"I'm sorry, Rose Bud."

I shook my head and held him closer.

Helicopter rotors whirled in the distance. *No*! It sounded like the same chopper Chena's men used to find us. Down the hill, the wailing of sirens echoed from the valley. One way we were saved, the other probable death.

"Chena must've discovered the watch had a blank USB flash drive," I said.

My father looked at me with a faint, wistful smile. "That's my girl," he muttered.

"Come on Teddy," Max said. "We need to get you up." He grabbed hold of my father's arm on one side. I took the other with my restrained hands.

"Thank you, Max." I shot him a tight smile. I genuinely meant it. I also knew if we weren't murdered by Chena and her goons, Max would be sent back to prison. I'd often thought if our lives did not turn out the way they did, would we have been together? We were tight as children. He was my first crush and best friend. But just as we stood on either side of my father, we were on opposite sides of the law.

We held each other's gaze. He gave a nod as if he knew he had to let me go.

Max and I watched the chopper draw closer. My heart pounded faster. I hoped the sirens would make it first.

Just then, the van went up like a roman candle. I put my head down to dodge flying parts.

My father suddenly released our hold on him and stood tall. "Get down!" he shouted.

Rio emerged from behind the burning van and aimed his AR. "You're not getting away that easy," he roared, dragging his charred body, peppering us.

Everything was in slow motion again. He threw himself in front of us, taking the fire, using his body as a shield. I fell, my body recoiling with every familiar sizzling dagger sear through me. My ears were ringing wildly.

The shooting stopped. Rio approached at a shuffle with his AR trained on us. To finish us off, up close and personal?

As I lay on the earth, I glanced over. The lifeless bodies of Max and my father lay next to me.

I reached a hand to my father.

He stared back, tears streaming down his face. He mouthed, *I love you*. His eyes glazed over, and his head sagged to the side.

CHAPTER 56

The chopper landed. Its occupants spilled out and opened fire on Rio. Who were they? Sand crunched beneath footsteps approaching at a run, and a familiar voice rang out.

"Shit ... they've all been hit ... Rose ... Rose," Kevin shouted, his voice trembling.

Out of nowhere, Sue Dog was next to me, whimpering, licking my face.

"Lily, get the dog out of here." Kevin's voice and others were now more muffled.

I wanted to say it was "Okay," but I couldn't speak. The world around me gave way. I had the sense of déjà vu. This time it was different, somehow. I was buoyant and soared as more emergency service vehicles arrived. They rushed to the three of us.

Out of nowhere, I heard a woman scream. I was moving at warp speed, like in a sci-fi movie. I stopped sharp and hovered over a hospital bed.

"Push Saki ... come on, love. One more ..." It was James's voice.

"Arrrgh." The pained sound of Saki echoed, followed by the cries of a baby.

"You have a healthy baby gi—"

Just like that, I was gone at lightning speed again. This time through a bright, warm, blissful tunnel. Now this was familiar. I felt myself smile as I came to a halt. I searched for the human-shaped light figure, but He wasn't there.

My mother emerged. She wore a white flowing gown and was gliding away with a man. I couldn't make out his facial features. I knew who he was and wanted to thank him for sacrificing himself. But they vanished.

Bradley swiftly arrived and embraced me. *Rose Bud. It is time to move on. We will all be here.* I heard his whispers.

"No. I'm home and want to stay, please," I said.

Suddenly, He appeared and spoke to me through my thoughts. *Soon, my Child.*

A quick, painful jolt surged through me.

"We got a pulse. She's back."

CHAPTER 57

A month later.

I sat by my mother's favorite bench, at the Key West City Park, eyes closed, as the ocean mist kissed my face on this humid, June day. It was high noon, and the white blazing sun was directly above, not a cloud in the sky. The only saving grace was a slight wind that had picked up. That and my flowing off-white flowery, sleeveless sundress I wore. Mom would've been proud, I dressed like a girl for a change. It was mostly out of necessity since putting on pants posed a challenge for my healing body.

The pooch lay belly up next to me, tongue out as the palm trees swayed in the sea breeze. She was probably exhausted from chasing snowy egrets on the beach. It did little to cool her, but she looked as if she enjoyed it. It was a no brainer to keep her, and I no longer had to call her "Sue Dog," just Sue. I think my friend would've approved.

Sue refused to leave my side and when they kicked her out of the hospital, she sulked and went on a hunger strike. So, my loving family did what anyone would do under the same circumstances. They found a service dog vest for her. It was a win-win. Sue is currently in training to receive the real deal. I always knew she had it in her.

We had a reason for sitting at the park at high noon in the heat. As I found it the most appropriate place to hold his service. We spent a lot of time here as a family. Not to mention everyone I knew moved to Florida, except for Grandma and Lily. You couldn't pry them away from Montana, excluding this weekend. I, on the other hand, was still transient.

"Rosie, today was perfect. It was nice of you to do this," Saki said, sitting next to me on Mother's bench. She smiled and cooed at the new addition to our crazy team, *Violet Rose Lee Powers.*

"When someone saves your life, it's what you do. I didn't know what to say. It's hard to pay reverence to a man you don't know." I moved my wheelchair to face Saki.

"Let me do that, dear," Heidi crooned as she adjusted my chair, locking the brakes.

"Always the nanny, Heidi Zimm. You'll never stop." I smiled.

"It's my calling. And you are supposed to take it easy," Heidi said.

"You know I can walk," I replied.

"Yep, but it's only been a month and you've broken your pelvis and arm, dislocated your shoulder, and don't get me started on your broken ribs." Kaylee ambled over to me. "Shall I go on? It's a good thing your stubborn head was unscathed," she said.

"Don't forget shot multiple times in both arms, Dr. Sis." I snort-laughed. "But who's counting. Thank God for Grandma's new ballistic shirt." I rubbed my chest.

I watched Grandma Lil and the guys carry on at the gazebo. I only imagined the stories Grandma was telling. She always had people in stitches.

As I returned my attention to the sea, I inhaled a deep meditative breath and exhaled slowly. "Do you think he would have liked the service?" I asked.

"I honestly don't care if he would've liked it or not. He did nothing for me," Saki said.

"Now Saki, that is no way to talk about the departed," a male voice responded.

Saki looked over her shoulder. "I'm sorry, you are right, Dad."

Our father rolled up in a wheelchair, with Lily pushing him. Uncle Tubbs close behind. Both of his legs were in a cast. He smiled widely at his three daughters.

"Whether or not you cared for Max, he sacrificed his life for the two of us. I guess he realized he was going back to prison and wanted to redeem himself," I said. "He had a sad life. Deep down I felt sorry for him. All that money and no one to love and spend it on."

"Except for you, Rose. He had it bad," Saki said. "Is that why you held the service at this park?"

I turned my chair toward the park. "We used to play here. I'm not sure if you know this, but he carved our initials in the gazebo."

Just then a black Town car rolled up, taking two parking spots.

"Someone is late to the party," Kaylee said.

"I'd say. And check out his parking job. Who does this guy think he is?" Saki said.

A man popped out from the rear driver's side. He was dressed in a soft blue collared shirt, tan suit, and a striped tie. He marched toward us with a purpose, swinging his briefcase.

"Excuse me. Are you Rose? Rose O'Brien?" he asked with a strong New York accent. The man was tall with a thin, athletic frame and his greenish-blue eyes were hidden behind wire-rimmed glasses. He was handsome in a Clark Kent sort of way. Just as he reached his hand inside his jacket pocket, Kevin, Tubbs, and James were on him.

"Easy buddy. Let's see your hands." Kevin jumped in front of me with his hand on his holstered Glock.

Sue joined Kevin and stood next to him.

Since Chena and her men were in the wind and SJ, among others, looking at hard time, Kevin, James, and Tubbs took it upon themselves to protect me. I let them, for the moment. But they should know by now I was always armed, and my threat level was generally on red alert.

"It's only a handkerchief," he said, pulling it out, wiping the sweat from his face and chicly styled black hair. "But I ... I need to speak with Ms. O'Brien." He stepped to his left and peeked at me.

"Who are you? What are you doing here? This is a private function." Kevin blocked the man again.

"It's vital that I speak to Ms. O'Brien." His tone was sharp.

"Stand down, O'Malley, I got this," I said. "I'm Rose O'Brien." I stood and nudged my self-appointed bodyguard and new companion out of the way. "What can I do for you?"

CHAPTER 58

The man set his briefcase on the grass. "Boy, you are a hard woman to find. I tried your home and place of employment. Your employer informed me you took a leave of absence." He removed his jacket and wiped the nape of his neck.

"What do you want with Ms. O'Brien?" James chimed.

"I'm an attorney, um, but I need to see some ID before I can discuss this issue with you."

"You first." I squinted.

Grandma joined us and sat on the empty bench opposite Kaylee and Saki.

He handed me a New York driver's license with his business card.

I studied it. "Okay, Mr. Keith Fenner, *Attorney*. What's this about? Am I being sued?"

"Nothing of the sort. But I have something for you and need to verify your identity." He shot glances around the group. "It's confidential. Can we go somewhere private?"

I eased back in my wheelchair, pulled out my badge wallet from my handbag and handed him my driver's license. "This is my family. I have no secrets from them." I shot him a cheeky grin.

"Not anymore," Saki mumbled, almost under her breath.

"May I?" He motioned next to Grandma.

"Sure," I said and wheeled around, facing him.

Mr. Fenner handed me a large manilla envelope that read, *Ryan Trust.*

"Normally, this kind of business is handled in my office … but nothing about this client has been *normal*," he said.

"What's this?" I asked with furrowed brows.

"Maxwell—uh, Max Ryan never discussed this with you?" Mr. Fenner inquired.

"No." I kept the answer brief. The attorney didn't need to know the history between Max and I.

"Well, you must have been someone special to him. He left it *all* to you." The attorney grinned.

I opened the envelope, pulled out a document, and keys dropped out. My mouth hung wide. "I thought the feds seized all his assets." I looked at O'Malley. "Kev, your two favorite words, 'Asset Forfeiture.'" I smiled.

Kevin shrugged and smirked.

"You are correct, however, not *all* his assets. As you know, he was a genius with making money clean and a good amount was legit. From his uncle and his mother's foundation. Oh, and those keys are for his Delta yacht and helicopter. Bought with clean money," the attorney said.

I could not blink or utter a word. I signed the documents and returned them to him.

"Make an appointment with my office and we will get the rest settled. If you need an attorney, I assure you I am quite capable and handle things discreetly," he said with a wink.

"Thanks, Mr. Fenner, but everything I do is on the up and up."

Lily chuckled.

I shot her a side look. "With my finances." I assume she was snickering about our escapade in Montana.

I turned to my father. "I don't think I'm going to need the Falcon money." I blew out a sigh and returned my gaze to the sea.

Mr. Keith Fenner from New York quietly slipped away.

"Why would he leave it *all* to me?" I asked.

"He had no family and probably no friends, and you were the closest to him," Grandma said.

I pondered. Not only did Max take a bullet for me and Dad, but he also left me his entire fortune. If Max had the love of family, would he have been happier? Money didn't save him. But it could certainly buy me the best physical therapy. I examined my shattered body.

"You're in deep thought, Granddaughter."

"Just feeling blessed," I said.

"There is so much to be grateful for, people forget that," Grandma said.

We all nodded in agreement.

I watched as James stepped up to Saki. She handed him the baby. He gazed into his daughter's eyes and back at Grandma. "So, I'm thinking we need a new name for the family protocol. Seeing how 'Violet' is taken."

We laughed and agreed. Hopefully, we would not need to use it. But you never know with the Reagan/O'Brien/Powers Family.

"Rose, what are your plans, now that you're rich? Will you return to work after you recover?" Kaylee asked.

"I thought they wanted you to medically retire?" Lily said.

"Medically retire?" Saki snorted. "That's an excuse to get rid of their number one problem child. Rosie is too much for them to handle," she said with a scrunched nose.

"But won't you miss wearing the badge?" Kaylee asked.

I opened my wallet and stroked my badge. "A wise woman once told me this badge does not identify me, family does." I closed my badge wallet for the last time and smiled at Grandma Lil.

"Well, if they don't appreciate someone with your discerning tactical skills, and who grabs life by the b—" She made a fist.

"Language! Grandma," Saki said as she covered Violet's ears.

Grandma pulled a twenty-dollar bill from her pocket. "I was going to say 'boys,'" she said with a chuckle, handing it to Saki.

Grandma Lil and I held each other's gaze. "Someone will use your skills." She gave me a wink. "I have a feeling we haven't seen the last of you, Rose O'Brien."

CHAPTER 59

Six months later

I sat on the upper deck of my newly inherited Delta Superyacht. I'd contemplated selling it and getting something smaller, but it accommodated my growing family just fine. And heck, it was paid for. Anyway … back to my happy ending.

I rested my head on the chaise longue meant for two, closed my eyes, and offered my face to the Bahama sun. I listened as Sue chattered with her new dolphin buddies as they rode and played in our wake. I pondered over the broken chain of events that led me here. Grandma Lil said it was God testing me. I have to say, it was the hardest exam in my life.

Just as I removed the sarong that covered

my mostly healed scars, the sliding glass door from the salon opened and closed. It was Kevin O'Malley. He had two Vodka tonics in hand.

"Merry Christmas, Red. The chef said lunch is served." He set the drinks on the side table.

I gave him a full raspberry and smiled as he eased next to me.

"Christmas isn't for another week ... and are you ever going to stop calling me, Red?" I put my head on his shoulder.

"It suits you." He kissed my nose and chuckled. "But, you know how you say my two favorite words are 'Asset Forfeiture'?" Kevin said.

"Yeahhh?" My voice went up a note.

"You're wrong." He stared into my eyes. "They are 'Rose O'Brien.'" He pulled me closer and gave me a long, lingering kiss, until Sue squirmed between us, smiling, wagging her tail.

I gazed at these two. My heart was full. My lone wolf now had a pack of her own.

THE END

AUTHOR'S NOTE

As a dog lover, I wanted to pay homage to my two fur babies, Saki, and Rose. Instead of writing about dogs, I bring them to the human world by creating characters from their unique K-9 personalities. This story is dedicated to all present, past, and future fur babies.

List of characters and their K-9 identities.

Rose   Saki

Kaylee

Titos

Lily

Bruno

Chena

Copper

Mia   Teddy

Gretel   Angus- a.k.a. Black Heart

Heidi   Rio

Tubbs

Toby

D.O.G.

Vino

Walter

Archer

Simon Rae

Stanley James- a.k.a. SJ

Olive- a.k.a. Butterfly

Bo-a.k.a. Sergeant BoBo

Elly May

Max, a lab mix, was a childhood pet. Pic unavailable

Last, but not least, Grandma Lil. She is the only character based on an actual person, my mother-in-law, Lillian Weinstock. Lillian was the inspiration behind Grandma Lil, and she was just as spunky as her fictional character.

RIP LILLIAN E. WEINSTOCK

ABOUT THE AUTHOR

S.S. Duskey retired from law enforcement with over 20 years of experience. She resides in the Bitterroot Mountains of Montana with her husband, Steve, and fur baby Rose. Rose and her late canine companion, Saki, are Sharon's inspirations for writing, not to mention her adventures throughout her career.

When she is not plotting mischief for her characters, Sharon enjoys spending time with her family, friends, and furry children in the outdoors of the beautiful Bitterroot.

Sharon invites you to contact her at ssduskey@yahoo.com or visit her website www.ssduskeyauthor.com.She can also be found on Facebook at www.facebook.com/ssduskeyauthor.

Note to Readers:

I hope you enjoyed reading my stories as much as I have in writing them. As an indie author, reviews can have a tremendous impact on reaching more readers like you. So, if you liked *Redemption in the Tahoe Basin* and any of the other two in the Rose O'Brien Trilogy, please visit Amazon and Goodreads and leave a review. Thank-you!

Made in the USA
Middletown, DE
29 July 2022